Fanatic Surviving

Dove Strong Trilogy #2

Erin Lorence

Fanatic Surviving
COPYRIGHT 2019 by Erin Lorence

Contact Information: titleadmin@pelicanbookgroup.com

Cover Art by *Nicola Martinez*

Watershed Books, a division of Pelican Ventures, LLC
www.pelicanbookgroup.com PO Box 1738 *Aztec, NM * 87410
Watershed Books praise and splash logo is a trademark of Pelican Ventures, LLC

Publishing History
First Watershed Edition, 2019
Paperback Edition ISBN 978-1-5223-0229-2
Electronic Edition ISBN 978-1-5223-0217-9
Published in the United States of America

Dedication

To the real Savannah, who would offer her last water bottle to anyone in the desert.

Your loving heart inspires me.

Dove Strong Trilogy

Dove Strong
Fanatic Surviving
Sent Rising

1

Thunk. Gilead's blade sank into the X scratched on the pine. Dead center. A breath later, Micah Brae's steel nicked the trunk's bark and scuttled, disappearing in the frozen groundcover.

My brother's grunt of disgust reached me up in the crow's nest where I huddled out of sight. "Pathetic, Brae. Keep your knife horizontal to your target until you release it. Like this."

Thunk.

I focused on the sunlit branches overhead instead of my brother's and neighbor's knife-throwing session—their way of preparing for the Reclaim. The war's first attack on the godless Heathen was broadcasted for May 15, a month and a half away. And they thought this would make them ready?

Next to me on the snug lookout platform high in the maple, my grandpa surveyed the tree-filled horizons in his systematic way. I leaned my elbows back on the woven blanket, evidence he'd slept up here, despite the biting Central Oregon nights. My mom said he slept in the tree to be extra cautious—with the war between us Christians and Satan's people approaching. But that wasn't the real reason. Grandpa was obsessed with sighting his missing son, my Uncle Saul, who I'd discovered back in September, alive, crazy, and nearby, roaming the Oregon Cascades.

"If Uncle Saul wanted to come home, he'd have done it years ago, Grandpa. You know that, right?"

He grunted.

My frown fell on the barkless, white pole in the distance. A dead tree with an eagle's nest on top, marking the corner of our property. Next to it ran the rutted path on which Wolfe Pickett had driven me home. Wolfe, the Heathen teenager I hadn't seen in six months, two weeks, and five days, who'd changed my mind about the nonbelieving population.

My frown deepened into a squint.

Under the third bleached branch from the trunk's bottom, a woodpecker had whittled out a bird-sized hollow. Did another note wait for me there? Could I check before sundown without my family noticing? Wolfe had already left me two secret messages in this hole.

Hey, Dove. I'm better and up for a visit. How about next Saturday? Su casa. Let me know. Wolfe

And then...

Dove, I know you got my note. Is this about the bean plant I killed? Tell me when it's good for me to come see you. No killing this time. Wolfe

I'd taken the notes but left no response. *Stay away, Wolfe.*

He wouldn't shed any more blood because of me. Last September my brother had stabbed him on our property for hugging me. Gilead would have killed him if I hadn't blurted out that I loved this unsaved guy and his intense little sister, Jezebel.

I rested my warm cheek on my knees.

So what if I loved a couple of pagans from the town of Sisters? Didn't *love* mean I didn't want them to die? At least the Spirit reassured me it was fine to love nonbelievers even if my family didn't applaud this.

"Being equally yoked in marriage is God's will, Dove. It's biblical. You marry a lost soul, and you'll bear a burden you won't be able to carry."

"Amen," my aunt had agreed.

Why did my mom keep blasting me with this spiel? Marriage? How dumb. I was only seventeen. Gilead's nineteen. Had she ever cornered him to give the "equally-yoked" talk? I was willing to bet my year's quota of honey-roasted squash she hadn't.

I grabbed a promising pinecone and cracked it against the platform. After a few taps, its nuts knocked loose.

"Here, Grandpa. Eat."

With a grunt, he picked out a couple from my palm. We sat in the sunshine, chewing and spitting hulls while knives clattered and thudded below. Maybe this squirrel food would hold my stomach until dinner. Then I wouldn't have to leave this hidey-hole or my grandpa, the one family member who never referred to my unexpected relationship with nonbelievers that kept me awake at nights.

"Dove!" My cousin Trinity's voice sang from close by, no doubt from inside our tree home, since it was too clear to be from the junk piles. "Dove, Gran wants you!"

Grandpa extended his hand for the rest of the pine nuts. Making sure not to knock against the giant emergency bell that hung within reach above our heads, I climbed on branches to my home's larger platform.

Once in our main living space, I took a backward step toward the open doorway. I should have taken my time in the branches and not rushed to get here. I took another step back.

My grandma faced me, spider-web fragile in her willow chair. Mom stood behind her, clenching the chair's straight back, an odd, tight smile pulled across her sun-stained face.

I braced myself for the marriage spiel.

Gran heaved herself to her feet, revealing bulkier homespun apparel than what she usually wore to shuffle around on the platforms. "Dove, child, go find your backpack. We're going to fix the blasphemous mistake. God wants peace and not war. He knows it, you know it, and I know it. We're heading back to the mountain to get it straight with that Council. Obey, child. I have no time for your gaping at me. Go get that pack so we can leave."

The mountain? The Council? My past failed mission came crashing down so hard I staggered.

Last summer, I'd been commissioned as God's messenger for peace. I'd traveled to Mount Jefferson, Oregon's Christian Council, and carried my family's and a next-door neighbor's prayer votes for peace. And on September 15, the fifty Councils had tallied America's Christians' votes. Despite my best effort to obey God, a decision for a war we called *the Reclaim* had been made.

A human mistake. God didn't want a war.

Before I'd left last summer, Grandma's vision revealed me reaching Mount Jefferson, and my own dream later showed the importance of halting the startling red that flooded the nation. I wasn't brainless. I knew what the growing crimson color meant. The red meant massive bloodshed—specifically our people's blood. And as God's special messenger for peace I should have stopped this bloody threat by getting to my Council. But my journey's successful arrival at the mountain with votes, my arguments against violence with fellow messengers, and all the hours on my knees among other prayer warriors hadn't stopped it. The Councils had announced war.

And now I had to make the trek again.

I glanced over my shoulder to the green, fuzzy canopies beyond our property and then squeezed my eyes shut.

Travel back into the devil's territory? My hands shook. But not because I was scared of his attack. Satan would strike—using snakes and hunters to do his evil deeds— and I would handle them. Bring on the snakes! No. I trembled because of a secret knowledge—an unknown threat—that kept me awake at night.

Lord, there's a pull I'm too weak to fight, even wearing Your armor. Part of the world out there draws me—like a heaping pile of compost draws a fly. Will the pile collapse on me this time? Trap me so I can't escape? Will I choose not to escape? Is that what happened to Uncle Saul? Almost eight years ago, he left on the same journey to the Council. Maybe I'll end up haunting the nonbelievers' roads and towns too...maybe Sisters? Will I never return to my family if I leave?

Should I tell Gran no?

I sighed at His reply. My feet traveled two steps forward.

"Yes, Grandma."

2

"You murderer! Look at your hair! You massacred it." Trinity pounced and gathered my now collarbone-length strands into a short tail and attempted to coil it. I'd left the rest of my blonde hair on the floor near my hammock next to the ancient scissors and family mirror.

I sniffed. It didn't look that bad. But I glanced down at the factory-made blue pants and black, zippered jacket I wore. Should I have not...?

I squared my shoulders, which were weighed down with my bag, and returned my mom's and aunt's stares. "It's smarter to blend in out there. So we're not spotted and attacked so easily."

I spoke the truth. My last trek into enemy territory had taught me the safety of blending in. Not that I was about to offer to search the junk pile for some castoffs for my grandma to wear instead of her homemade clothing. Or suggest she cut off her long, coiled hair like I'd done.

Mom drifted nearer to me, holding out her hands. "Dove. Daughter. You want to be a...camouflaged Christian? And look like a...a worldly woman? I don't think it's wise—"

A *thump* sounded, and I crossed my arms.

Gilead stepped onto the platform trailed by Micah. "Whoa!"

A crowd of chattering, little-boy cousins swung in from different limbs. At least my grandpa, following in back, didn't react to my changed appearance. Instead, he scowled at the black radio dangling from his hand. The bottom half was missing except for some wires, which he jiggled so they danced. "Radio. Seems to have got broke. Somehow."

I shrugged. Other than the initial news of the Reclaim date, our radio hadn't announced anything worth hearing. The radio had been a gifted provision from the Council to each departing messenger so families could receive important information and stay united. It blurted out news of sporadic attacks cropping up in Portland, where I assumed the Christians who broadcasted were stationed. Last week a believer hurled a rock into an enemy's truck. The projectile had struck the pagan driver and caused the vehicle to flip. But the radio reported no more Council news.

Gilead slouched closer. "The radio was the first casualty of war. My bad. Almost as bad as...this." He flicked my zipper and started to hum.

Micah, glancing at me every third word, stuttered about how the electronic got crushed during his and Gilead's sparring practice. It had been an accident. A freak gust of wind that had knocked it into their path was the real culprit. And all the while, Trinity watched him with a satisfied smile, as if she'd finally discovered a person too perfect to improve upon.

I gagged behind my palm. How could my talented, artistic cousin fall for our skink-boy neighbor who'd shown up a few months ago and wouldn't leave? But I'd spotted her newest piece of artwork at our garden's perimeter. The sculpture depicted a familiar, angular face with dark, Brae irises and spider-leg lashes.

Grandma cut Micah off with a slashing hand motion. "Gilead, you do realize that this demolished radio is our only communication with our people about the Reclaim? This is no humming matter."

He jerked up as if surprised at her scold. "What's left for us to know? We attack May 15. That's what the radio people said."

"Don't be so sure, Grandson. Dove and I are going to see that the decision is changed. We're heading back to the Council at Jefferson for the true ruling, and it may take us longer than mid-May to return. So how will you know what to do come May 15?"

My brother's brow cleared. His lip twitched—almost a smile. "If God wants me not to fight, then He'll have you home before the fifteenth with the good news. Or He'll fix the radio. I still have faith, Gran. Even if some of your other grandkids have lost theirs...and want to dress up like Jezebels." He knocked my zipper again.

I bit my tongue because Gran brought her knuckles to her hip. "Gilead Jonah Strong. You will not fight in sin."

We Strong kids don't argue with the adults, but Gilead did...and almost crossed the line of disrespect this time with his typical, pigheaded fierceness. He wouldn't be the only Christian not to fight on Reclaim Day. Gran and I would make it home before then with a changed answer if God's will was for peace. He wouldn't even agree to wait for us in case we were a few days late.

In the charged silence that ensued, my aunt whimpered. My grandpa stepped forward with a straighter spine than was natural for him and cleared his throat twice. But what could he do? If only he was the powerful grandpa he'd been years ago. Back then, he could hold both me and Gilead in place with one arm. Or if only his son, Jonah, had lived. If he hadn't been murdered, my dad would still be scrappy enough to knock some sense and respect into my hulk of a brother.

"You're a lamebrain, Gilead." I moved to the top of the ladder and began to climb down. "But it's a deal. We return with the Council's new answer for peace...and you lay down your knives and leave the godless alone. Now come help Gran down so we have a chance to get there and back before you make yourself a dead lamebrain."

~*~

Mount Jefferson filled the horizon faster than it should for an arthritic old woman and a homesick seventeen-year-old. How had we come so far in four days? Last August it'd taken me weeks to get this close.

The painstaking length of that summer trek must have been Melody Brae's fault. Melody, Micah's twin sister and the Braes' family messenger, empowered with her spiritual gift of being ultra-alert to danger, had led us on zigzagging detours through the farmland and high desert country. Her panic had dragged us off course and wasted time.

But I wouldn't lie and pin the whole difference in journey on Melody. My grandma and I weren't making a pit stop at Mount Washington this time for a

Christian "warrior" to accompany us. We would stay far away from the mountaintop villagers—or MTV—and avoid the closest town of Sisters with all its godless citizens, including the Picketts.

"Good," I told the cicadas' electric buzzing in the sagebrush. "The last thing I need is to run into Wolfe or Jezebel now."

"Amen." Four shambling steps ahead, my grandma picked her way straight through the piles of red lava rocks, as if following an invisible beacon.

"Keep away from the unsaved, Dove. Especially the male ones. I always knew you had brains somewhere in that skull of yours."

My toe scuffed against the rocks, and I faltered. "Well I don't plan to pick up any males of our kind either, Gran. The last ones about killed me."

She didn't reply. She probably understood that I referred to Reed and Stone Bender, the macho Christian brothers from last September who'd tossed around violence as easily as throwing around pinecones. Although Stone had disobeyed his warrior brother's last orders to silence me. And he'd made a kind offer...

I trudged toward the snow-capped peak. It towered as a sky-reaching reminder of how I'd failed my last mission of peace, of how the prophetic red grew. I glanced behind, eastward, toward home.

"What are they're doing now, Gran? At home?"

"Praying."

"Even Gilead?"

She didn't reply to my stupid question. It was daylight. He'd be running drills and doing target practice.

"You think we'll make it home with a new

decision in time? To stop him and Micah from attacking?" Why couldn't I shut up?

My grandma plunged into a stream's weak current without seeming to notice it. It was the only response I got.

3

Governor Ruth, the silver-haired leader of the Oregon Council, waved at us from the slope's crest. Behind her lone, cloaked figure, the dense forest continued to climb until defeated by higher crags and snow.

My body slumped, and I exhaled until my lungs were empty.

Thank You.

God had taken care of my impossible problem of how to get Gran to the Council's quarters. The last stretch into the hidden crevice included rock climbing with ropes and possible rappelling. But instead of providing us with ropes and super-human strength, God sent the person we'd come to meet to us in the foothills. I tried to picture the woman tottering toward us with her arms spread wide, making the climb herself. I couldn't picture her.

"Oh, my Sarah. My Sarah," said the woman.

Millions of wrinkles flowed across both faces as they hugged. The governor guided my grandma to a mossy log.

Gran motioned to me. "Dove, this is my childhood friend, Ruth. We've known each other a long time. Together we survived the chickenpox, failing the fourth grade, and later on...persecution." From her tunic, Gran pulled out the half-heart necklace she always wore, touching it to the ornament Ruth lifted from her own neck. The two charms made a whole heart.

"Uh-huh. I remember the governor." I moved away from their weird display of kindergarten affection to find a decent tree to rest in. But first, I'd scout in case anyone else lingered in this part of the Jefferson wilderness.

This part of the forest was silent and still. The various tracks from human feet etched in the mud and grass were days old. I kicked a skinny trunk. It wasn't as if Melody and Stone, who both lived here at the Council, had known I was arriving at their doorstep. But I'd sort of...hoped? I'd hoped that God had whispered something to them, and they'd be here.

Dumb, Dove. Few people bothered to listen to God the way I did. Plus, we'd made our relationships clear on our last day together in September. Melody had rejected me when she'd refused to travel home with me. And I'd rejected Stone by refusing his unexpected proposal that we stay together forever.

I quit kicking downed limbs and wandered on...thinking about a hand that broke skull-sized chunks of lava rock into pieces. A hand that had reached for mine.

I ran my fingers over my cheek muscles, erasing my dumb grin.

A few-yards' meander brought me into an unexpected, property-sized clearing—the type of clearing Heathen make with their bullying machines while desecrating nature. But they weren't responsible for this one.

Hundreds of heavy feet had trampled the ferns and grasses around the axe-hewn stumps. A smoky tinge clung the area where target cutouts shaped like human bodies leaned against taller tree remains. With a glance at the empty tree line bordering the clearing, I crept toward a chopped stump. My bloodless fingertip traced a bullet hole.

I whipped up straight, my palms beginning to sweat. This was a training camp. The kind Gilead dreamed of. The bullet holes announced that the believers training here for the Reclaim had moved past knives and clubs to more deadly, forbidden weapons.

I recognized Warrior Reed's work. This spot testified to his passion for violence and vengeance on a large scale. He wouldn't be satisfied training up a handful of soldiers. He'd want hundreds. Maybe thousands.

A shadow of his battle cry echoed off the evergreens as it had that night around the campfire six months ago.

"Brothers and sisters in Christ. A heavy satanic force descends. The time has come to defend not only ourselves, but our land and our Council. Our enemies dare to attack us on this land set aside by God for His people. So I charge you to be brave. Be bold. Be the first believers to fulfill the Reclaim to take back our land, starting with this mountain."

I backhanded the target, knocking it from its perch. Riddled with holes as if termite damaged, the flat wood burst into fragments on the dead weeds. I destroyed four more nearby targets, kicking the pieces to sawdust before moving back in the direction of my grandma.

Gran must've heard the wood splintering, but when I approached, she didn't look away from her friend.

"We've a better chance now than ever before, Sarah," Governor Ruth said. "Our leader on Jefferson who has been gifted in strategy and fighting has motivated the others across the nation. We're leading our nation's uprising in a way I never thought possible. The troops' zeal is relentless. But there's unrest and disagreement across the nation, too."

"You question your resolution for war? You feel it was a mistake?" My grandma's eyes bore into the councilwoman's.

"Yes." Governor Ruth hesitated. "And no. We Council leaders believe God calls for war—but a different type. A spiritual war. The vote was too close last fall—divided straight down the middle, half for peace and half to fight. We leaders were staggered by the number of young delegates called as messengers. We'd never seen anything like it before. And we believe the tied vote...and the hordes of young messengers...are a sign."

The governor unwound her arm from her cloak and pointed it at me. "The young believers. We feel God wants them to come out of hiding and to mix with the pagans. To live among the godless and teach them God's truths."

"No!" My grandma banged her walking stick against the ground and struggled up. "No. Not among Satan's people. Not to live without family."

"Our youth are strong enough, Sarah. God has His reasons. He wants them—we in the Councils understand that now. And I won't question His decisions or authority."

"Then you believe we made a mistake? During the Purge all those years ago, you think believers shouldn't have gone into hiding? Better to have stayed and been persecuted? Killed?"

Governor Ruth lifted her bundled shoulders. Both

wrinkled faces turned my way.

My grandma's gaze traced my zipper and dropped. "Her?"

"I believe God has chosen her. She will be a leader in this movement. She's already Heathen-inclined."

I ran down the slope to a giant cedar. Sheltered in its limbs twenty feet up, I peeled needles from a bough and waited for my grandma and her pal to stop discussing me. To finish talking about me being a leader in a movement among the Enemy's people. In the back of my mind a voice whispered. *Rejoice. Be happy. They decided on peace instead of war. Gran was right.*

I repositioned myself and twisted again, unable to get comfortable on the limb.

I'm not strong enough. Please don't ask me to do this, Lord. Don't choose me again. I'll only fail. Remember last time?

The two women mentioned Saul. Then they discussed how the new Reclaim decision must reach the believers at the secret broadcast station in Portland before May 15.

None of that mattered. Uncle Saul had made his choice to wander among the godless, and careless boys had broken our radio. My brother's life expectancy depended on our return and not a radio broadcast.

I covered my impatient lips with a cluster of green and watched the birds alight and take off at will. Light and burden-free.

4

Gran's face glowed tired in our campfire's light. I'd gathered moss and ferns for our bedding on the earth where, come dawn, the inevitable chill would creep into our bones.

I surveyed the deciduous foliage above my head. If only I could somehow get her up into the tree tent for a decent night's sleep. But it was impossible. I was no Gilead, and she couldn't make the climb.

I sighed and weeded the empty plastic bottles from our packs. "I'll get water. You rest."

She nodded with shut eyes. Deep shadows under her eyes made her look a thousand years old.

I cut through the darkness and moved in the direction of the stream we'd passed earlier, taking my time and listening for bats. I was used to nighttime forests and the critters that roamed them, so I didn't freak out over the small rustling noise in the bushes a few feet from where I stooped to collect water. I stood up...and knocked into a body looming over mine. I couldn't help it. I shouted.

A light flickered, illuminating a skinny guy about my age with a wimpy, brown beard. He held a flashlight. Water from the uncapped bottles in my hands left dark trails down the front of his leather shirt. His hazel eyes laughed at my shock.

My fingers dented the thin plastic with a *crack*.

"Reed!"

"Dove."

"Holy Moses. Apparently being creepy is your newest weapon." I gripped my bottom lip with my teeth while my heart thudded.

The warrior showing up like this? It couldn't be good. Not for me. The last time we spoke I was positive he'd ordered his brother, Stone, to kill me in revenge for messing up his plans...and because I'd taken a stand against him and his bullying.

Why had he hunted me down tonight to surprise me at this stream? Was he here to carry out his old plan of revenge? *Oh!* I'd destroyed his targets this afternoon. He must have found out.

I pointed to my right, in the direction of the far-off training camp. "I'm not going to apologize. I only put a few out of their misery. The targets were used up, ready to split anyway."

Confusion replaced his smirk. Then he shook his head. "Give them back."

"Huh?"

With a jerk, he tossed my bottles to the ground, splattering water across my shoes. "You know who. I'm not naive, Dove. They disappeared the night before you showed up in this wilderness. I may not know how you three have been communicating all this time, but I do recognize your power over them. They wouldn't abandon me without you leading them. So give them back."

I blinked twice. "Are you talking about Melody and Stone? They left you and ran off? Together?"

I wasn't sure what was worse. The chilling way Reed drilled me with his unblinking stare or the disturbing vision of Melody and Stone, hand-in-hand, prancing out of the Jefferson wilderness to share a life somewhere.

His Melody. With my Stone.

My lips twitched, and I laughed. Hard. In his face.

The warrior retreated an unsteady limp backward.

"Why not, Reed? Why couldn't they go? Unless you and Melody got married? No, I didn't think so. Your loss then. Next time, propose before your brother does."

"He hasn't. Anyway, they're mine. He's my brother. And she's my...Mel."

Keeping my eyes on him, I gathered my tossed bottles, now empty. "Can't help you, Mr. Insight. I know nothing. Apparently about as much as you do."

He blocked my way to the campsite and held up two fingers. "Two days. If you haven't returned them to me in two days, then neither you nor...is it your grandma? The one taking the nap back there? Anyway, neither of you will reach wherever you're headed."

I pushed past, trying not to run, refusing to act scared.

He hasn't hurt her. He hasn't. There'd be no point in him hurting her.

"I don't know where they are. Do you see them with me? Where would I be hiding them?"

"Then why are you here?" On this mountain?"

I clamped my lips together and glared. I didn't have a death wish, so I didn't blab about the different Reclaim decision we'd come for.

"You've got two days to return them to me."

I stalked off with my chin high and left him and his unfounded threat by the stream. Once the lazy rush of water faded out of earshot, I bolted.

The warrior hasn't hurt her.

I skidded to a noisy halt next to the glowing embers. My grandma slept, unhurt, breathing soft and slow. I added more sticks to the charred pile and plunked down onto the dirt. I reached my cold hands to the refueled flames.

Neither Reed nor I had mentioned the changed Reclaim decision—that the war was to be a spiritual fight rather than combat with weapons. But did he know? He was a leader at Mount Jefferson now, so if he hadn't heard the news, he would soon. And when he found out, no doubt he'd blame me for ruining his war on top of stealing away his brother and Melody.

The truth of this gripped me, and I clasped my knees. He'd blame me, despite the fact I didn't hold the power to change a war or kidnap Melody...let alone Stone, a giant.

I rocked back and forth. And his threat...Well, what could I do about Stone and Melody? Nothing. And if Reed didn't believe me, and his ultimatum boiled down to hand-to-hand combat, I'd lose. Reed was as skinny as me, but he knew about violence, strategy, and winning fights.

My rhythmic swaying stilled. I gazed up at the patches of night sky between obscuring treetops.

Fear no evil. You are not alone.

My muscles grew warmer. The tension in my body oozed away, replaced by the heat from the flames. Positioning my balled-up tent as a pillow, I settled on the layer of ferns and moss.

I wasn't alone. I traveled with Grandma Sarah. Wise. Tough. Someone I could count on with the brain power to know what to do and keep us alive...and on track for home.

~*~

I sat up in the crisp, pearly gray. My tongue was like sandpaper and my lips dry as dust. Next to me, Gran's breath whooshed out in slow gusts. Movement jerked me around.

A blue jay.

I aimed a pebble at the feathered intruder exploring Gran's satchel and then gathered our water bottles and my grandma's walking stick. Its knotty weight felt comforting in my grip.

At the stream, I relinquished my weapon. Still, I couldn't fill the containers fast enough. My fingers fumbled in the icy water.

Quit being such a scaredy squirrel. But I shifted uneasily. Was I alone? I shivered and straightened.

"Come on out!" I filled the air with my authoritative voice. I'd called out because I needed to hear my confident tone—not because I expected anyone to obey.

A bottle slid from my grip when Melody stepped out from behind a cedar.

In six months, Micah Brae's twin sister hadn't changed at all. She was still tiny under her shaggy fur clothes, her deer eyes too big inside that pinched face, smudged and pale. Her sharp nose raised to sniff out danger. She was a human mouse.

"OK, Dove? Is it OK if I come home with you now?"

I clutched the remaining container to my heart. "You're only about six months too late in asking that one, Brae." I flicked my chin in a *c'mon* while trying to see behind her. I peered around at the surrounding trees.

She jogged forward. "No. Stone's not here. Only me. After he helped me down the rocks, he went his own way. Said he was going back to his village on Mount Washington."

"Sure, Melody. It doesn't matter." But it did. Stone had ditched Melody as soon as they reached the trees, which was quite different than the offer he'd made me—to keep me safe forever.

In the brief pause, she didn't mention Reed. I didn't either.

I reached out and threw my arms around her in a loose hug. When I let go, her huge eyes bulged in surprise. But last summer, she'd wormed her clingy little way into my life, and ever since I hadn't been able to shake my desire to protect her.

"Don't think this means I forgive you for what you put me through, making me tell your mom you weren't coming home. She cried on me, Melody. Cried." I shuddered at the traumatic, tear-stained memory.

She helped gather my bottles and knelt next to me at the stream, her thin fingers going white under the current's flow. "I'm glad you were able to stay alive to do it for me. Really glad. I'd been thinking you might not have made it home. Reed hinted a couple times you hadn't. But I know you better, so I told him. I told him that despite your way of spending time with those Heathen, you'd make it home to Ochoco. I told Reed so, but he wouldn't listen. But that's Reed. He never listens...at least not to me.

"So why are you here? Did you and Micah get married? Am I going to be an aunt soon?" She squinted at my jacket front and then at my left hand. "I don't see a ring, but that doesn't mean—"

I stood up, deciding not to upend the full bottle over her braid-covered skull. Though it would be satisfying, I'd have to gather more, and my hands were too numb. "No. I didn't marry your brother...or anyone. Why would I?"

She pulled a face and stood. "Oh, too bad. But whatever happened to that pagan guy and his sister? Walt and—"

"Wolfe and Jezebel. I don't know. I don't see them anymore."

She considered me with one eye squinted and a fist on her hipbone.

Why was everyone watching me all the time? And now with Melody joining her brother Micah, there'd soon be one more person around Ochoco to avoid. What fun.

She nodded. "Well, that's one piece of good news. Although you don't sound glad about not seeing them. But really, it's a good thing. Super good. You'll forget them...start dressing normal again soon...I mean, that was a relationship going nowhere—"

"Speaking of doomed relationships, what happened between you and Reed? I assume you broke up since he's not here holding your hand." I cut my snarl short without mentioning Reed's nighttime visit and threat at this very spot.

Melody trailed after me as I trekked back to my campsite. "I guess this is us breaking up. Don't you think? You think I should've left a good-bye note? Anyway, I doubt he's even noticed I'm missing with the mob always around him and the intense training he leads. He's so...focused. All the time. On his job. Fight! Kill! Conquer! It's like the Reclaim is his own personal war or something. And he's really good at what he does, preparing everyone and getting them pumped to fight—even believers at other Councils through satellite. You should see how they all respond to him, Dove. He's amazing. And he loves it."

"He loves it. But not you?"

"Well...he'd never love anyone as much as that, would he? What's for breakfast?"

Gran woke when I tossed a few sticks on the smoldering fire. "Saul?"

"No Gran. Only me. And Melody Brae, Micah's sister. OK if she travels home with us?"

She eased back down. "Of course, child. Welcome."

5

I scrubbed my toe in the dirt and erased the monster bobcat paw print. Behind me, Melody and Gran picked through the clinging bushes and ferns. Neither of them commented.

Good. They hadn't noticed.

I didn't frown because of the size of the print...but because it was human-made, drawn in the dirt by only one person. Reed. The owner of a giant bobcat named Darcy that he'd left behind at his home on Mount Washington.

The fake print suggested that Reed stayed ahead of us on our trek down the foothills. He wanted me to know it.

Instead of this cryptic warning, why didn't he come out in the open and talk to us? OK, fine. Melody joined up with me after his threat last night. So what? I wasn't going to tell her what to do—go back to him, a guy she decided she didn't want to court or marry after all.

The next sign of Reed's proximity didn't arrive until bedtime. While the three of us sat around the fire, hunched over our clawing stomachs and fantasizing we'd had more huckleberries than a handful each, a smoky aroma wafted over us. Meat. Salted meat.

Melody groaned and grabbed her belly. "That smells like..." Her eyes grew huge and staring.

Turkey vulture. A Reed and Stone Bender favorite.
I shifted into her line of sight. *Danger?*

She inclined her head. *Yes.*

Well, this was interesting. It seemed Reed had passed over to Satan's side if she registered his presence as danger now. No wonder she ran away.

I stood up, no longer afraid. Try to take her, Reed. Try to stop us. God is on our side. Who's on yours?

I moved over to my grandma. It was time I told her about the warrior and his threat to stop us. I'd planned to talk to her alone, but it didn't seem to matter now. If Melody considered him a threat, then she shouldn't get weepy over what I had to say.

"Hey Gran, I…"

She looked up with shining eyes. "Yes, child?"

My stomach lurched, and my motivation drained away. I understood the reason for those happy tears. In her mind, at a nearby campfire, Saul was responsible for the smell of cooking meat.

"Uh, never mind." I plopped down.

I couldn't crush her hope or add to her burden by announcing we were being threatened. Usually Gran was strong and could take anything. But ever since we'd left Governor Ruth, Gran seemed...old.

~*~

All three of us were alive the next morning.

I didn't gasp at the new footprints next to our burned-out ash pile, but I frowned that they were so large, with a tread and no sign of a limp. They weren't Reed's.

While the others slept, I scoured the terrain until I

discovered other tracks between the bushes. At consistent intervals, a pattern of three dots smudged the dirt and needles.

Uncle Saul wore machine-made boots with rubber soles. He also carried a three-pronged walking stick.

I knelt next to a dot trio made by his walking stick and surveyed the surrounding brush and trees.

Where was he? What did this mean?

Melody mumbled in her sleep, and with a sweep of my hand, I smudged out the marks. I moved to the campfire and watched the woods.

Saul had visited our camp and left before I woke. Did he miss Gran so much that he wanted to see her? Because if that was the reason for his drop-in, he should have hung around a bit so she could see him too. It was only fair.

A new energy filled me, and I hummed. I grabbed a branch and swept it over the prints around the fire.

Saul was near. He was family—my dad's brother. He wouldn't let Reed do anything to harm us. Good. Because our two-day ultimatum ended tonight.

~*~

"Sarah!"

The shout reached me...but had I heard right?

I followed Grandma out of the hemlocks and onto the edge of a flat expanse of farmland. Her expression remained focused, lined with exhaustion. I readjusted my gaze. Stay focused. Let's just make it home.

Then my nostrils registered acrid smoke. I halted and put a hand to my brow.

The muffled sun at the horizon illuminated a

collapsing hut ahead. A plume rose from the abandoned shelter.

My backpack absorbed Melody's stumble against me as the first orange flames reached out from the glassless window. They clawed upward at the caved-in roof.

Gran shuffled on without a missed step or a change in pace. As if still following that invisible beacon, she beelined for the small inferno.

I jogged after. "Gran! Wait!"

She paused at a tumbledown fence. Her veined hand picked up something from the weathered top rail and pressed it against her chest.

I stared at her tight fist. What had she found?

Her gray eyes pierced me, but she gave her command to Melody—a shadow clutching my pack.

"Turn around. Go back to the trees and hide. You'll wait until it's safe and then continue home. You're not to follow me." She clambered between the fence's warped wires.

"Gran, No! Where are you going?" I grasped her bony elbow across the fence, but she swung around with such force I released it.

"Dove, child! Obey me now. There's no time for this. Obey God. Let me go."

As if in a dream, I watched her march toward the flames, away from my still-reaching hand. She'd tossed her walking stick aside and stood taller. Her stride copied Gilead's at his fiercest. I held my cheeks in my cold fingers. This wasn't a dream but a sick nightmare.

"Dove." Melody tugged me backward by my jacket. "C'mon. She said hide. I feel it. We need to do what she says. Now. Danger. Hide."

I wrenched away, catching myself against the

tilted fencepost. Gran had disappeared around the shack's side and probably searched for a door, a way in. But why? I had to stop her.

Melody pulled again.

"Stop it!"

Without taking my eyes off the burning building, I stooped and picked up the small object Gran had let slip from her fingers...as if this clue could help me save her.

The half-heart necklace—the half that matched Gran's—dangled from my fingers. It was the necklace Governor Ruth wore two days ago.

The world ground to a stop on its axis. Reality became my heart ramming icy liquid through my veins, followed by a jolting flash of understanding.

My grandma believed she was on a rescue mission to save her friend who was inside. She didn't know this was a trap set by Reed. Of course it was. Fire was his favorite weapon. Why hadn't I told her about the warrior's threat? She was clueless about him and didn't know this was a trap—because of me.

I stumbled backward, dropped the chain, and let the Brae girl drag me back to the safety of the hemlocks. I fell to my knees behind the first bush.

"Farther, Dove! Keep moving back. Please move. They'll see you."

As the siren's wail swelled, Melody let me alone and disappeared in the forest behind me.

A red truck pulled up close and shot blasts of water at the flames. Where was Gran? Ruth? The roof crumbled and collapsed with the sound of shifting firewood.

I stood. "Gran!"

A chorus of sirens swelled, drowning out the

rushing water. Two cop cars bumped into sight, up a distant track, and headed for the giant bonfire. A trailing cloud of dust rose into the thick air.

Movement fluttered in my peripheral vision. An emaciated man in tattered rags poised motionless at the tree line about ten yards away. He appeared entranced by the flames.

I leaped toward him, pointing at the burned-down shack. "Saul! Uncle Saul, it's Gran inside. Help her, Saul!"

He half-turned, and the branches behind him parted. Seeming not to hear, my uncle melted back into the forest.

"Saul!"

I tripped, hunting for the space between hemlocks. Where had he gone? Why wouldn't he help me? Help Gran?

"Saul!"

Someone grabbed my arms and made me kneel in the waist-high weeds. The person shouted at me, forced me to my feet again, away from Uncle Saul and toward the fire. Past it. And into a gray car.

I wore handcuffs, identical to the kind my dad had when he'd been dragged off our property by the police years ago. Someone outside the vehicle still badgered me with questions, asking about the fire, saying I needed to cooperate.

I closed my dry, aching eyes and flopped back against the warm leather.

Reed had won.

6

I slumped on a hard bench the color of fish guts. They'd charged me with arson and manslaughter. I zoned in long enough to figure out that the Heathen accused me of setting fire to someone's property and killing someone. My grandma.

Except they didn't know she was my grandma. They called her "unidentified victim." And I was "unidentified suspect."

Fire Investigator—the name of the stranger who'd scoured the fire scene like a bloodhound out for actual blood—had picked up my pack where I'd left it at the fence. My bag...but not my stuff inside of it. At least not all of it.

According to Fire Investigator, my bag burst with incriminating stuff. A lighter, a fire starter, a plastic bag with lighter fluid residue, a firework wrapper, and a suspicious letter. I only recognized the fire starter—a piece of flint and steel.

Had Fire Investigator planted these things because he hated radicals? It was possible. But most likely Reed had done it while I'd slept last night.

I should be mad. Plotting bloody revenge. But nothing mattered anymore. Gran was dead. And Gilead would die too unless our radio got fixed, and that was unlikely.

A uniformed woman wearing a radio above her wide, bearish hindquarters rejoined Fire Investigator.

She loomed over me. "Things will only get worse for you unless you tell us your name so we can contact your guardian."

Worse? I squinted at the crack waving through the paint on the opposite wall—like the rolling hills near Prineville—until it went blurry.

Her snub nose grazed mine. "Listen. We know you're a radical. Or do you insist on calling yourself a Christian? It was a good try with the disguise, but we read the letter. We know what you are. We know what you people do. So talk."

I shut my eyes to her bugging ones, also blocking out the pink room and the orange pantsuit I wore. What letter? No, yesterday I would have asked about a mysterious letter. Not today.

I heard Fire Investigator's knees crack as he squatted. "If you don't start talking, girlie, we're going to begin rounding up every known radical cell within fifty miles until you're identified. And there's a lot of illegal activity going on with your people that we usually let slide. Is that what you want? Your whole family arrested too? Talk, girlie."

When I didn't answer, the woman decided for me. "Fine. We'll start with that radical cell just south of Mount Hood. Hmm? You belong with them? They're connected with an old arson charge. Even if you aren't part of them, fanatic, if we decide to raid they're bound to give us the locations of a dozen other radicals around here. No use tightening the noose around every fanatic's neck. Might as well tell us."

Fire Investigator's hot breath blasted my forehead. "Ochoco. Outside of Prineville. There's at least one group there. They have a cozy setup in the trees with zip lines and catapults."

"Yeah, that's right. We've had run-ins with them before."

"Is that your cell, girlie? I'm glad to follow up on the old charge of environmental terrorism—"

Pickett. Pickett. Pickett. An invisible source whispered.

"Pickett." I said. "Pickett." The name seemed familiar. With a burst of brainpower, I added, "From Sisters, Oregon."

The woman lumbered up, her thumbs hooked under her tight belt. "OK, Pickett from Sisters. You start thinking about loosening that tongue and cooperating like a good little terrorist while I go notify your family."

~*~

"Me being in here isn't funny." I glared up at Wolfe Pickett, who leaned against the other side of the bars and laughed.

"You won't be laughing, Wolfe, when I have Gilead slash another hole through you."

He leaned in so his triangular nose jutted through my side of the doorway. "Quit being so crabby. Or I won't pretend you're my cousin anymore."

"I never told those cops out there I was your cousin."

"Well they think you are—a cousin from the delinquent, fanatical branch of my family. My grandma explained it to them, which is pretty decent considering she has no clue what you're in here for, and she thinks you tried to murder me last fall. But she's a genius with an audience and loves a challenge.

She's convinced them so the guards are being supportive. They suggested we join a support group for people whose family members go fanatical. And look at this." He strummed a plastic card across the bars. "Free lunch voucher. Since they feel bad for me, having you as a relative."

His pupils strayed to my bare arms.

I crossed them, hiding my sword and shield tattoos. "I don't lie. I didn't say you were my cousin."

"Well I do...and did."

The one person in the world I didn't expect to see stepped into the room. Rebecca. My Christian ally who'd helped me defeat Reed and save Wolfe's and Jezebel's lives last September. Her God-given gift of convincing people to do what she wanted allowed her to live in the city of Portland surrounded by nonbelievers. This made her the one person in Oregon who could help me out of this mess, if anyone could.

She grinned lopsided at me. "By the way, this isn't jail. You're in a CTDC—Christian Terrorist Detention Center—though I suspect you're the only real Christian here. Mostly they house violent offenders in the center until they can prove nonreligious motivations. But what you'll care about more, Dove, is that I told the officials you're eighteen, so they'll stop searching for your real family. I assume the last thing you need now is for them to get dragged into this mess."

For a moment, returning her smile seemed possible. "How come you're here?"

Wolfe threw his arm around Rebecca's square shoulders. "My idea. Genius, huh? I thought I'd have to dig all night for her info, but she was too easy to find. She actually has a phone number. Did you know she'd won an award for super-smart chicks? And she's in law school at Lewis and Clark."

I shrugged. "Did you...you know—"

"Work my magic?" Rebecca held up her thumb in victory. Her thumbnail shined with paint, as odd as the fancy, worldly clothing she wore, complete with sticks on the bottoms of her shoes. And how did her bushy hair now hang straighter than mine?

I gripped the unyielding bars in both hands. "So, I can leave now? They believe that I'm innocent?" Of course they did. Everyone believed Rebecca. Even when she wore ridiculous shoes.

"Mmm. It's not quite as simple as that. You need to tell the officials the same things I already inferred. That the farmhouse was burning when you got there."

"It was."

"And that you've no clue who set it." She waited with a lifted brow. "And that you don't know the person who died."

I swallowed and studied my fingers sliding up and down on the bars.

Wolfe's tanner, warmer ones locked around them. "Your grandpa?" He swallowed. "That...stinks. I sort of didn't hate the old man."

I shook my head. "Not him. Grandma. My Grandma Sarah died."

"Well, Dove. You'll just have to lie," Rebecca said matter-of-factly.

I nearly agreed.

Wolfe threw her a side glance. "She won't be able to, you know."

She nodded. "I know. Even if she did, they wouldn't believe her. That's why we'll have to go with plan B."

"Wait." I jerked my hands away. "What?"

"Excellent. A jail break." He began examining the fit of the door against the rectangular opening. "I'll provide the EMP to blow out the lights and security—"

"No." Rebecca frowned at him. "If I'm here, we keep this legal. That's why you wanted me, right? As a legal representative?"

"You're way off. I brought you here for your brainwashing powers. You say bibbidi-bobbidi-boo, and our bird girl's free."

Rebecca turned her back on him. "So, here's the deal. No, Dove. Don't interrupt or I'm gone. Those people out there you're treating like enemies? They've agreed to drop the arson and manslaughter charges if you plead guilty to trespassing, which you'll pay off by participating in a two-week, work-release program."

I crossed my arms.

She grinned lopsided. "It's in Texas."

My nails bit into my inked shield.

"In the desert."

Wolfe dusted detention center floor grime from his hands. "What kind of work release program is in a Texan desert? Is the job trying not to shrivel up from heat stroke like people in survival TV shows? I told you about that one with fanatics from different religions, called Fanatic Surviving. And last week the Western Buddhist lasted only three days in some desert. Deserts are bad. Stay away from deserts."

He squinted at me. "Don't do it, Dove."

Rebecca moved to the bars, her grin gone. Her warm eyes fused with mine. *Trust me.* "Wolfe's being ridiculous. It's only for two weeks. All you've got to do is get through two weeks of this program. Show the nonbelievers that Christians are hardworking and tough. That you're not a coward. It's a good deal,

Dove. I'd do it."

Wolfe's dark head bobbed. "You should do it. Definitely. A good deal."

I nodded too, as suckered as Wolfe by Rebecca's persuasive words. Even though the last thing I cared about right now was what nonbelievers thought about Christians—meaning me—and whether I was hardworking or chicken or whatever.

"Yeah, OK. But," I clenched my hair. *Gilead.* "I don't have two weeks."

"It's two weeks or one year."

"Two weeks or one year," Wolfe parroted.

"Two weeks..." I reached out to grab my friend's wrist. "Rebecca, what aren't you telling me? I feel...no, I know you're holding back something."

She returned my clasp, squeezing until my knuckles creaked. "But you trust me anyway? Smart. I'll go tell your buddies out there we accept their bargain. Just keep being smart, OK? Sign the papers, plead guilty to trespassing, go along with what they say—without biting heads off—and I'll meet you in two weeks."

She raised a hand while turning to leave. "Stay strong, Strong. I mean...Pickett."

~*~

I survived the next two days in a fog of pink paint and orange stripes. A couple of females wearing the bright pattern shuffled past, their yells and shackle clanks jarring me into alertness. When it happened, the fog lifted for a few seconds, leaving my brain clear to dwell on my unwelcome reality. *They believe I killed*

Gran. Gran's dead.

On the second day, a stripe-wearing shouter shut in the room next to mine, further polluted the stuffy air with her crazy mumblings and outbursts. Wrapping the flat pillow around my ears did nothing to protect my brain. Instead, my fingertip traced the lines of my arm tattoos.

I should use my Armor from God. At least my shield and sword. But my arms—like my mind—were too heavy for such a huge effort.

Later. I will later. I flopped back to stare at the pink crack. In any case, Wolfe might be here again at any moment.

Wolfe met my shrugs and one-word retorts with laughter, although the amusement seemed off—forced and half a second too late. Did the weird vibe have anything to do with the notes he left in the woodpecker hollow and my refusal to write back? Or my hint that I didn't want him on my property? No, he wouldn't be so sensitive.

I stopped pretending to sleep and sat up. "Wolfe, what do you think I'll be doing in Texas?"

"Scraping flattened armadillo off the roads."

I bit my lip. That wouldn't be too bad. As long as the other workers scraping left me alone.

"And you know what, Dove? I bet they'll save the carcasses for you, so when your two weeks are up, you can bring the whole sackful home. Your family can make armadillo stew. You'll provide them with dinners for the whole spring.

"We don't eat roadkill for dinner."

He stood up to leave. "I wouldn't know. I've never been invited."

Oh. Maybe he was sensitive.

An unknown amount of time later—seconds? Hours?—I blinked away the fog. Jezebel stood within sight, though still on the other side of my door. She scowled up at the bear-hipped lady who glared back.

The dark-haired girl stamped her foot. "What do you mean I can't see Dove without an adult with me? Why do you think I brought this brother of mine along? Of course he's eighteen."

My brow lifted at this. I'd always known she was a natural liar.

Jezebel's small hand found her jutted hip. "Anyway, there's a law that people can visit their cousins anywhere, anytime they want. You need to go back to guard school and figure it out if you don't know that. Hey! You let go of me!"

As the red-faced guard marched her down the corridor, trailed by her laughing brother, small projectiles flew through the bars at me. Jezebel stuck her hand in her pocket and released another colorful handful that bounced like hail at my feet.

"Here's candy, Dove! Candy. Quick."

After she left, I tried to sink back into the pink haze. To not think of Grandma gone. Gilead waiting for me at home, sharpening his knives. Saul so unhinged he wouldn't save his own mother. Melody lost in the foothills of Mount Jefferson. My upcoming two weeks in a faraway, arid land doing who knew what type of work...

I zoned in on the crack in the paint, following the rolling sprawl until a guard turned out the fluorescent bulbs for the night.

~*~

"ON THIS NEXT EPISODE OF *FANATIC SURVIVING*—"

I awoke and bolted upright. My body cringed against the cement wall, my chest heaving. A rectangular, bright screen blared at me from the other side of my bars.

"Shut up! Shut up. Shut up... shutupshudupshudup..." The orange-striped mutterer next door had woken too. "She gets a TV? Gimme one too! Only terrorists get the good stuff around here? Fine, I'm a terrorist...who'll send you all to Hades if you don't gimme a TV! Gimme...gimme..."

I positioned my back to the movements on the screen with my arms curled over my head. This electronic screen with its glass front was identical to the ones stacked in rows at the Council last September. So the uniformed people in charge wanted me to watch this one? Why? As a punishment? The mutterer didn't seem to think so.

Either way, I wouldn't watch. No one controlled what I did with my eyes and brain but God and me.

But my arms and the skinny pillow couldn't block the booming sound. After a few minutes, I peeked. With a sigh, I sat up. It was easier to zone out on the screen than cracked paint. And my annoyance at the incessant noise and changing pictures kept my mind off thoughts that jabbed me like a tagalong porcupine.

After the short bout of yelling, my neighbor quieted down. Some others who'd called for the electronic to be violently destroyed copied. Listening, I guessed.

On the screen, the woman swathed in black fabric scraped a hole in the dust with a flat-edged rock. Sweat from her covered head dripped between her worried eyes. Sudden, bold red words interrupted her quest for water in the wasteland. *FANATIC SURVIVING.*

So this was the television show Wolfe had mentioned.

I moved to the bars and glanced up and down the empty corridor. Someone in this detention center had an off sense of humor. Or was plain evil. Forcing me— a fanatic—to watch other fanatical religious types suffer in order to survive.

I poised at the edge of my bed and bit my thumbnail for the sweaty, dehydrated Muslim-looking woman on the screen.

She failed.

After she gave up, a new episode began. A man named Aadesh in a Hindu-type of white turban began his survival in a jungle.

My nose wrinkled. Compared to the woman's, a jungle was a super-easy environment, and the guy wasn't using his trees at all. He deserved to fail. But the narrator didn't point out the guy's lack of basic common sense.

"The second day ends, and Aadesh is still unable to obtain the basic resources of water, food, and shelter needed to sustain life. So, his journey comes to a harsh end. Is his failure rooted in the fact that the spiritual power he bases his life on is a lie? Is his God too weak to provide? Or is his downfall merely due to his own lack of faith? Perhaps, the reason for his inability to survive the harsh jungle terrain is grounded on all three."

A new black-capped human began his episode...

The screen flickered. *Vroom!* A herd of bright, sleek cars snarled past on an oval of pavement. I knocked against the cement at my back and blinked up at the blonde standing next to the screen, holding a tray of food. She shoved at the wheeled electronic, rolling it to the left and into the corridor out of sight.

"My turn. About time...time..." My neighbor's mutter became lost in the engines' screams and an excited voice from inside the television.

The blonde clanked my door closed behind her and banged down my breakfast on the floor. She studied me.

I studied her back. Who was she? Her hair was cut a lot like mine, which I'd done with rusty scissors, but her clothes were factory made. The disgust on her face told me she wasn't a fan of Christians.

I sat up straighter and tilted my chin.

She jerked a thumb at where the electronic had been. "Two hours are up. And that was her deal for you."

She answered the question that must have leaked from my narrowed eyes. "Rebecca's deal. She requested you'd receive two hours of television time prior to your hearing. Plus, all meals delivered to your cell and that the officers leave you alone—no more questions. Oh and a quick arraignment. And you get your possessions returned after you stand before the judge. Rebecca's good. I would never have gotten them to accept even half those demands if it'd been me bargaining for a radical. But you've got me now, and I'm way more than you deserve, so stop glaring. You're still pleading guilty to trespassing?"

I nodded.

"Huh. Fix your hair. You'll eat when you get back." She tossed me a plastic comb. "And if you're wise you'll do like Rebecca told you. Follow my lead, sign the papers, smile like you're grateful, and get on with your wasted, radical life."

The guard lady entered and shackled my wrists and ankles without touching her skin to mine. When I offered to hand back the comb, the blonde passed it to the guard between two fingers as if it were a rotting mouse carcass. "Toss it."

As the three of us headed down the hall, we passed the electronic on wheels. It fell silent. The blonde's stick shoes clicked with confidence. The guard breathed heavy at my back. And my enraged neighbor cursed God because her television time had ended.

7

My orange-striped clothing clung to me, all damp and sweaty. For hours, I'd gripped my tattooed forearms, waiting for the dead-eyed judge's verdict. Now, as the thin lips parted, I leaned into God's presence, a solid force surrounding me.

The judge made his ruling. Two weeks. Work release program. Southwest.

He slammed out of the room. The evil, electric cloud that hovered all day disappeared behind the wooden door.

But wait! What would I be doing in the work program? He hadn't said.

"Go ask him!" I poked the blonde—my defender named Savannah—and pointed at the judge's exit.

She stepped out of my reach. "Papers, Pickett. Let's go sign. Back to your cell."

My sweat had dried by the time I finished scrawling my false name—Dove Pickett—on the pile of papers I'd been commanded to sign. I handed the last one on the clipboard to Savannah and rested my head against the coolness of my cell's concrete wall.

"Fine. Here you go, Pickett." She held out a fabric bundle.

I leaped up and grabbed it. They were new clothes made with brown material.

The tunic and pants were made of shaggy fur like the kind Melody wore. I held them up high and let them drop to the floor. "Is this a sick joke?"

She sniffed. "Pick up your outfit and put it on."

I toed the furry mass away from myself. "No. I wear these, and I'm marked. I'll be running for my life the whole time I'm in Texas. Every single person in the program will know I'm a Christian. I'm not wearing these."

My public defender clicked out the doorway and banged the bars shut behind her. "Go in your underwear, then. I'll have someone fix your hair in the morning before you leave. If we can't get a bun out of it, we can at least try a short braid."

Her footsteps faded, and the lights went out. My neighbor's voice yelled six times for me to shut up before it eased into its mumble.

I moved to my mattress. In the weak, artificial nightlight from the corridor, my backpack slumped on the bed as if defeated. I settled on the mattress. Its sharp, plastic tears poked through my thin orange pants. Hugging my bag to my chest, I inhaled the scent of woven fibers. Dirt. The dried berries I'd shared with Gran and Melody.

For the first time since being arrested, I wondered about the Brae girl. She hadn't been apprehended, or she'd be in this Christian Terrorist Detention Center too. Had Uncle Saul helped her? Or had she run into Reed and been marched back to the Council?

Reed...had Reed watched my grandma fall for his trap? Had he seen my arrest?

I gripped my pack tighter. Then I relaxed my hold and opened its floppy edges.

Home overwhelmed me, plugging my throat.

Inside waited my familiar tree tent and patched blankets. When I pulled them out, the metallic material caught the faint light with a flash and crackled. I tensed and watched the cement wall, separating me from my neighbor. No one yelled for quiet.

I plunged my arms back into the pack, discovering my empty water bottle and tubular bee call. The bee repellant was missing a glob from its middle. No doubt the cops had taken some and tested it to find out if it was an explosive.

I upended the bag and shook it onto my lap. No clothes fell out. And my fire starter was gone. They'd probably confiscated it so I didn't burn down the detention center. The lighter and other objects Reed or Fire Investigator had planted to make me look like an arsonist were gone too.

With another shake, an unexpected, folded-up piece of paper wafted onto my orange-striped leg.

A letter. The letter? The one the female guard had spoken of?

My heart throbbed in my throat. I pulled the paper open. Writing covered most of it. The scrawl wasn't Reed's handwriting, like I'd expected. It was my grandma's. I gasped.

Jumping to the bottom of the page, I read the signature. The message was from Governor Ruth, whose handwriting mimicked Gran's. I slumped and read from the top of the paper.

March 25ᵗʰ

To: Rahab's Roof PCB (Portland Christian Broadcasting)

Importance level: Critical

Announcement: A new Reclaim consensus has been reached by the nation's fifty Councils. A unanimous decision has been made for a spiritual conquest. Note the change in the Reclaim from a physical to a spiritual nature.

Warning: *Those listeners choosing to disregard this missive will not be supported by the Oregon Council.*

Further Call to Action: *On May 15, each Christian household will send at least one family member into a local, non-Christian populated area to live for a year. These Sent will attempt to coexist peaceably with nonbelievers. The Sent will bring no weapons. We are challenging these believers to rely on the Spirit to guide them against the Evil One and his workers, whom they'll encounter living in his territory.*

Note to Rahab: *This is an ASAP broadcast that you will announce twice daily until May 15, the set date of our spiritual Reclaim. Importance level is critical so that all Christians within Oregon's borders will hear and know the change of action.*

Governor Ruth L. Graham, Oregon Council

To ensure the authenticity of this directive, compare handwriting for forgery and only accept if delivered by the original messengers. Messenger One: female. Eighty-two years of age, five foot three inches, with an identifying scar running wrist to elbow. Messenger Two: female. Seventeen years of age, five foot seven inches, with a full body tattoo of the Armor of God. Do not let hostile demeanors influence your trust.

The governor's words swam across from the creased page. Shock slid from my scalp to my toes, numbing every cell in its path. I closed my eyes but still saw the curving scrawl.

Not again. Oh, Lord. Please no. Please, let me have made a mistake!

In the gloom, I forced myself to reread the last bit about the messengers. No mistake. I was messenger two with the full-body Armor of God tattoo. Messenger One with the scar was Gran, dead and at peace in heaven.

This put the full burden on me of delivering the message that would stop the Christians in Oregon from attacking Heathen.

If this radio broadcasting station in Portland didn't receive the changed plan written on the paper that had drifted to the grimy floor at my feet, then they couldn't inform all the families who'd been given radios last September at the Council. That meant thousands of deaths. Massive unauthorized bloodshed spreading across Oregon against God's will. It was up to me to get to Portland with this critical announcement.

And I headed to Texas in a few hours.

I began to shake.

Why hadn't Gran told me we were delivering this message to Portland? Why had she even accepted the commission? By doing so she'd chosen the lives of strangers over Gilead's—her own grandson and my brother. She'd chosen to spend our precious time hunting down this secret broadcasting station instead of going home to tell him.

Had she even known how to find this place? Rahab's Roof? Because I sure didn't. I'd never heard of it.

I closed my stinging eyes and pictured her following her invisible beacon without hesitation.

I shook my head. She hadn't known where Rahab's Roof was located. She hadn't cared. She'd trusted God to lead her...and she'd expected me to do the same.

Anger flared. My eyes teared and burned. I leaped up and kicked the cement wall. Pain shot up through my toes into my ankle.

"No," I rasped.

I glared at the creased paper on the ground and reached for it.

New plan. I'd tear it into a million pieces and shove the whole mess through the tiny holes in the detention center's metal vent to the outside world. God wanted this message to get to Portland? Fine then. He could use the wind to blow the message to His recipients. I was done delivering.

Paper in hand, I moved to the wall's vent above my head. I eyeballed the small openings and ripped a blank corner off the paper. As I peered up at the holes, a star appeared.

I froze. The corn-kernel sized, wadded-up paper ball dropped from my fingers, forgotten. I breathed deep and continued to watch the tiny prick of light in the night sky.

I shifted my head and found another star through a different vent hole.

Stars shone—hundreds of them. I hadn't seen the stars in days. Because I hadn't looked up.

I loitered, chin up, eyes glued to the vent. I shifted my weight back and forth to relieve my aching soles.

"Sorry, Lord."

When I couldn't stand any longer, I slid to the floor beneath the rectangle. I wouldn't give up my view of the sky and the comfort of God's closeness. The temporary warmth of a loving hug that'd held me in the courtroom when evil swirled enveloped me again.

I patted around for the torn page with Ruth's writing. I folded up the paper and eased it into my sock.

Yes, Lord. I'll deliver it.

But first, as soon as my two weeks were up, I was going home.

8

I opened my heavy lids. The bright sun shone while my toes skimmed the top branches of familiar maples.

Oh. I was dreaming. I'd had this dream before.

With crossed arms, I waited, alone, for the red to start dripping.

Plop, plop, plip. The bright color welled up over my home's roof, my garden, and covered the Ochoco green to every horizon.

The dove made its predictable appearance. When the creature took off, I pursued. Because what else could I do? I couldn't float about in this bloody forest alone, waiting for my family to reappear when I knew they wouldn't.

The red spilled over the land below as the white tail feathers passed over. There was something I needed to do. What was my mission again?

Right. To catch the bird. To stop the red. Except I knew what would happen because I'd attempted this before.

I would fail.

But the first mountain, where the dove paused, was different—not Mount Washington. Instead of black, volcanic rock, the tan, flat-topped cliff rose up. Crumbling sediment covered the landscape, and baked dust parched my throat. Where was water?

Oh, yeah. My mission. I reached out my tired arms

to grab the departing bird, but I missed it. I jogged a few steps, only to land in a puddle of maroon. The metallic liquid splattered my lips, and I gagged. Then I shook myself off, flinging red droplets.

In the heat, the stain on my clothes evaporated so my brown layers weren't drenched in red. Instead, flecks of white covered the animal skins I wore.

I was morphing into the dove. Time was running out.

I launched myself, every cell in my body and mind reaching after the bird. With the decision, a burst of strength flooded through me, driving out exhaustion.

Like an eagle, I soared up beside the winged creature. I could reach out and grab it anytime I wanted. But why? Where was it headed? I should hold off catching the culprit until I found out where it was going...its destination could be important.

Instead of capturing the cause of the red and heading home, we flew on side by side. Together we rose higher, past a moon that glowed crimson and through a shower of falling stars.

An ugly, gray slab rose in the air before us, almost as high as the moon. With one hand touching the slippery feathers beside me, I touched down on the tower's concrete top. Shorter, rectangular slabs crowded the one I perched on, which was higher than the rest.

The dove strutted to the tower's edge and began to coo.

A rumbling cut off its call. The solid concrete at my feet became liquid. I shoved up, using my white feathery wings to save myself.

I, the dove, soared higher. Looking down on the red I'd helped spread.

9

The small plane shuddered and lurched. My insides copied the flying machine's movements, and without thinking, I threw out my arm.

Three strangers in the cramped space shifted away from my gesture. Two others recoiled as if I'd been trying to hold their hands. The idiots.

I lowered my arm and clutched the snug strap at my waist.

Savannah, who'd surprised me by coming along on this ride, reclined in the chair across from me. She continued to peer down her nose at me with a curled lip. Disgusted that I appeared so much like a radical now? Or that I didn't look radical enough? Why did she even care?

Sweating in my thick, brown furs and pieced leather shoes, I knew I looked weird. Worse than Melody, who wore clothes like these. Of course, she'd never had a fake hair coil glued to the back of her head.

In the next few seconds of smooth flying, I knocked my skull against the back of my chair. The pulling strands hurt my scalp, but the coil loosened.

"Mess it up and the next one we attach is twice as big." My public defender unzipped a black bag next to her, offering me a peek of something the color of my hair but shaped like a small bees' hive made of braids.

She gave the bag a pat. "It's not a threat. It's a fact.

It's all we've got."

I left my hair alone for now and rested my forehead against the plane's oval window. The scene on the other side of it stayed dull. Everything below was dusty brown, both the flat stretches and shadowy bumps. We hadn't passed over any boxy shapes—shelters—since I'd finished my water.

I peeked at the five pagan strangers in the seats next to and facing me. They wore clothes similar to the ones I'd camouflaged myself in when I'd traveled with my gran. A couple held electronics like Wolfe's. The youngest, whom I first guessed to be Trinity's age but then decided was older than Gilead, kept black plugs in her ears. All pretended to ignore me. All hated me. An evil energy sparked and ebbed inside this space.

My sweaty palms scrubbed against my fur knees. I spoke loudly to be heard over the noise of the plane. "Are some of you in the work program, too?"

The girl with earplugs bopped her head in a random way, not in a meaningful response to my question.

"Then are you people all prison guards? Or cops? Officers?"

Next to me, the small, swarthy guy with handsome features laughed. He reminded me of Wolfe...except much more unlikable.

I unlatched the belt at my waist and stood, awkward in the cramped space. My neck bent in a way it wasn't meant to, but I stayed on my feet. "Answer me! Who are you? Where are you taking me?"

Across the way, a balding man with little neck leaped up when I did. Before he could react more, a bump in the air knocked us both back into our chairs. Everyone quit pretending and glared at me.

I returned Savannah's, which after a few blinks, lowered. Victory. Did that mean I earned an answer? "Tell me. Tell me who's at this work program and what I'll be doing—"

The engine kicked up an octave, drowning me out. The glarers shifted, tucking papers and electronics back into sacks.

I swiveled toward the oval window. The ground drew nearer, but besides dust, all I could see in the sunlit dullness was a helicopter. It rested on the dusty beige ground below. Still no shelters appeared. No wire fences containing crowds of people wearing animal skins.

My hope faded—the hope that they were taking me to a work program for captured radicals like myself. A place where furs tunics and hair coils were the norm.

A Christian camp was better than the alternative, a program for criminal nonbelievers who hated God. People who would make me suffer while we...while we did what? That was the other question. The question whose explanation must've been in that pile of papers I'd scribbled on without looking at them.

Dumb me. Dumb Rebecca. Why had she told me to smile, sign, and go along with everyone? Why hadn't she stuck around and gotten me answers?

Obvious. Because she already knew the answers. Like my Gran, she thought it OK not to tell me important information I needed. *Just trust me, Dove. Trust me.*

The plane screamed. Either the noise or the air itself plugged my ear canals. After a few earlobe tugs, I stopped. It didn't help anyway.

To keep from clawing at my hair and ears, I

reached down and pretended to scratch my ankle. The paper my grandma had accepted from Governor Ruth without telling me remained stiff under my thick sock. Hidden and safe. I rested my temple on my kneecap. The girl with the black earplugs watched me through almond-shaped eyes, as if I was a freak she was trying to figure out. She bopped her head when I watched her back.

I braced myself as the plane bounced and roared to a stop.

Welcome to Texas.

~*~

As I exited the plane, I looked up at the pale, wide sky. I stepped wrong and fell to my knees onto the faded desert. For a couple of blinks, the gravely dirt bit into my palms. Savannah was behind me, and I scrambled away from the plane's steps so she didn't impale me with her stick shoe. She didn't wear boots like the rest of the group.

Wherever we were going must have been a bit of a hike because there wasn't anything in sight except a helicopter that perched like a giant bug over faded green tufts. I doubted we could all fit on that vehicle.

The foreign, empty landscape spread in all directions with a retina-burning brightness. But the sun didn't scorch and wouldn't cause heatstroke...unless a person was idiot enough to wear fur.

A light breeze brushed the sweat on my temple, and I closed my eyes.

When I opened them I still stood in the middle of nowhere. Texas. More than a million miles from

Oregon and the places I needed to be.

The motley group of Heathens unpacked a staggering amount of baggage from the plane, which didn't seem so small now. In the distance, some choppy-looking rock hills flowed. A couple cacti struggled. No trees...

I reshouldered my worn pack and left the plane's shade.

"Hey, Pickett!"

With my back to Savannah, I balanced on a lava rock the same color as everything else. Then I jumped and kept walking, even though I'd no clue where to find the work program's shelters.

"Wait for your directions, Pickett."

I covered a few more feet of the crumbling terrain before halting. If she was ready to address my questions, I might listen.

When I about-faced, I bumped into the Earplug Girl, though they were gone from her ears now.

"Watch it!"

She had Melody's dark features, but her response reminded me of Diamond, the Pickett's neighbor from Sisters. The girl had hated me enough at first meeting last summer to hunt me through the wilderness in order to attack. There was a familiar tensing of the wiry arms. A widened stance. And since her footsteps had been as silent as a cat's, I would be sure to keep my eye on her.

The short man with Wolfe's tan skin and dark hair—my neighbor on the plane—laughed again. Not a nice laugh. But the others around Savannah hushed up and kept shoving things into the containers on the ground. I glared at every human on my way back to Savannah.

When I reached the plane's shade, she pointed in the exact direction I'd just walked, except her finger motioned further out at the large, choppy rock structures on the horizon. "Remember to head south, as you agreed to do in your contract."

She drifted for the helicopter. The guy who'd been throwing bags and boxes onto the ground shadowed her. He positioned himself behind the vehicle's glass, half-bubble window.

I threw up my arms. "That's it? Sky alive! Why don't you tell me what to look for? A building? A sign? A path to follow?"

"You're kidding. The radical doesn't know!"

The exclamation had burst from behind. The speaker was the same girl with the narrowed, almond eyes who nearly stood on my heels.

I took a couple of deep breaths. "You know where? So I follow you, then? Fine, whatever. As long as you know where you're going. I don't want to be stuck out here lost and wandering."

The girl's mouth dropped open, and she raised the heavy-looking electronic. I hadn't noticed it before. Was it a weapon? A type of gun? A whisper of panic clawed at me. I fought the sudden urge to plead.

Just tell me. No matter where I'm heading or who you are, it can't be as bad as not knowing. Please. Spit it out.

Savannah climbed into the helicopter and paused with her head and neck sticking out from the curved glass. "I really thought you'd have put the pieces together, Pickett. I'm disappointed in you. Are all radicals so naïve?"

I clutched my bag's worn strap, retreating backward as if slapped.

She shook her head. "Rebecca said to wait and tell

you when we got here, but I was sure you'd figure it out before now. I was wrong. I hate being wrong."

She lifted her black glasses and squinted, not against the sun but in disbelief. "You're a radical Christian. You're in a barren land. You're surrounded by a camera crew. You've signed a pile of agreements and waivers with the name of the show all over them. *Fanatic Surviving*. Ring a bell?"

I stumbled back another step. What was happening?

I charged the helicopter.

10

Two men in short sleeves blocked and threw me backward, rejecting me like a rotten, worm-eaten tomato they didn't want to touch. A man-made wind overhead ripped at my clothes and hair and blew dust in my face. I turned my back to its source.

The almond-eyed girl pointed her camera at me.

I glanced at the silent plane to my left. Then I rotated to face the giant rock formations. I was the new contestant on *Fanatic Surviving*. The whole enemy world would watch the new religious freak, struggling to stay alive in a desert. They would judge my God and my faith by how well I did.

I lurched over a tufty thing and stumbled on.

The wind lessened. The beating hum in the sky faded, carrying away the person who'd sidelined me. But her warning still boomed in my ears, words I'd heard but hadn't comprehended while I'd twisted and fought to get past the muscled men.

"You've two weeks to fulfill your sentence and contract. Reach civilization in Big Bend National Park in South Texas on day fourteen, and you'll find your ride home waiting, which, of course, will be us. Oh, and Pickett, you fail or give up—for any reason—and the deal's off. Breach of contract. You'll finish your term in prison."

My first reaction after I'd stopped struggling was to refuse to play this crew's twisted game. I'd sit at their plane's steps for however long it took them to understand I wasn't someone they could trick and manipulate. But then I'd heard the voice.

Two weeks or one year.

Strange. The Spirit's warning had never echoed Wolfe before. Or Rebecca. But I knew for certain if I followed my stubborn instinct, I'd spend a year locked behind bars, gazing at peeling pink paint. One year. Not two weeks.

I made my choice.

The moment I left the plane's shade and headed south, a steady calm ambushed me. Like the herb paste my aunt brushes on bee and nettle stings to numb the pain, the calm numbed my brain.

I didn't plan. Didn't feel. Didn't worry about the girl at my back...the cameras...what the pagan would see on their screens. I only moved under the open sky. Picked up my foot. Put it down. Side-stepped the dying cactus. Avoided the critter hole by the acorn-shaped rock.

My calm coma wore off by the time the sun began to set. I'd traveled so far south, I'd reached the tumbled rocks at the base of larger, column-shaped boulders. Without the sun, my sweat grew cold, and the chill slapped some sense back into me.

I was being careless. From now on, I would pay attention or I might step on a rattler. And what else lived in this unfamiliar wasteland? Besides snakes, there could be a million creatures Satan might use to stop me from getting back to Oregon.

Because I would get back. *I promise, Gilead.*

I didn't turn to face the others when I spoke. "I'm going to sleep. I want to be alone."

"Good night, terrorista. Sweet dreams." Laughter

ensued.

I scurried up onto the boulders, keeping my hands and feet out of suspicious, shaded cracks that could harbor critters. No footsteps or echoes of rock fall followed me.

Near the top of the pile, I searched for a hollow I could fit inside to rest. The chosen site would hide and shelter me yet provide an escape exit in case a predator visited. My head swiveled in the direction of the humans below. I didn't trust them, and I couldn't shake them off.

Or could I lose them? Out climb and escape them? What were their abilities, anyway? I hadn't paid much attention to them today, except for the girl who'd stayed with me as if we were connected by a short piece of rope.

I lay on my stomach on a flat spot next to a jutting boulder. With my chin on my fur sleeve, I studied them.

This time she hadn't followed me. She was still down there below making camp with the others—all men. A couple were sort of huge. Gilead style. Guards? Here to protect her and the camera crew from my fanatic violence? Well, they didn't seem scared of me now.

Through the laughter and calls, bright tents appeared...and so many supplies.

I sat up and opened my pack. My tent stared up at me, a useless pile of material without trees to hang it on. I dug under it for my metallic blankets. Before wrapping them around my body, I held up my water bottle to make sure there weren't any drops inside.

None. But my fire starter had been returned. At least I wouldn't die of frostbite.

I threw my collection of belongings down for a head cushion and checked for Ruth's message. The paper still lined my sock. I settled down. The stars began to pop overhead. My left hand traced the familiar, soothing constellations. My right gripped a pointed rock. I would survive *Fanatic Surviving*...or at least make it through this first night alive.

11

I awoke and touched my nose. Not numb. My body uncurled from its cramped ball while the sun's rays spilled over the edge of the horizon where chasm met stacked plateaus of rock. No sounds came from the sleeping camp below.

I needed water.

I stayed still, thinking of the people I'd watched on *Fanatic Surviving* and how'd they found water.

The turbaned guy had encountered no problem in his jungle. It'd rained and poured. The guy after him, the one with a brimmed cap and flowing beard, had been in a desert with palm trees, but there'd been a stream. Lack of food had gotten him in the end. I'd just thought him too wimpy to kill what he needed for nourishment until words flashed on the screen, explaining his god didn't allow him to eat certain foodstuff—like rabbits, pigs, and bugs.

Odd, because those were the exact resources that'd stampeded through his palm-treed oasis. The herds of roaming boar had seemed suspicious to me. What would the creators of this show throw at me to keep me from surviving? What was to be my personal struggle as a Christian?

Easy. Lack of water. Gilead's teachings spoke in my memory. "You can go three weeks without food, Dove, but only three days without water. Three days. So, keep your water bottle full."

Wearing my backpack, I crept over the sky-reaching rocks in the opposite direction of the colorful tents below. I scoured the terrain, searching for slashes of green vegetation, anything to indicate water.

No green.

I slid down the rocks to the flat expanse of beige.

There was a muffled, slithering *thud*. I whirled and stared into a camera. The girl wielding it sidestepped in a circle, apparently to keep me as her focal point. "So you're Pickett, huh? Pickett from Sisters? What if I say you're lying?"

I turned and faced the south horizon. She scuttled around to keep in front of me.

"OK, Pickett. Tell us. Does your God require long hair? And aren't you thirsty? Why do you have nothing to drink?"

In an automatic gesture, I touched my head. My bun had become off kilter in the night and now hung crooked. My other hand held my empty bottle. A surge of annoyance shot through me.

She spoke into a smaller device at her wrist. "Pickett moving southwest."

The liquid canister hanging heavy from her belt sloshed and swayed. I swallowed with a thick sound.

She covered the liquid canister with her hand and lowered her camera with a self-satisfied expression. Her body tensed as though she was preparing to do battle. Like Diamond.

Did she actually think I'd fight for her water?

A man's shout brought my head back. A man's form crouched on the rocks above.

"Jessica! You are not to engage with the fanatic alone! Ever. I don't care whose kid you are. Do it again, and I'm calling for your ride out of here."

"Whatever."

Before the sun fully cleared the horizon, the whole group circled like vultures. They kept their distance, but never strayed too far. Yet they were easy to ignore, staying out of my direct path and intent on their bulky equipment.

Soon the rock formations petered out, opening up to the flat, barren terrain. I kept a sharp lookout. Low spaces might be riverbeds that held rain runoff. Animal prints could lead to a water hole. Green bushes often hid secret stashes of liquid at their roots.

This desert held none of these things. Nothing but the same stupid pointy plants everywhere and some lizards. And I wasn't desperate enough to chase lizards to locate their water sources. Not yet.

~*~

By afternoon, I began to follow lizards. I stalked them with shaky knees, a clenched stomach, and a pounding headache that made strong thinking impossible. How had I thought this wasteland wasn't hot?

At the next boulder, I collapsed in its shade. I flopped over, facing away from the two cameras converging on me. Overhead, a helicopter beat past with a quick, gentle rhythm.

Energetic footsteps crunched over and stopped next to my ear. White teeth grinned down at me. Wolfe? No. I squinted through the heat. The tanned face was a few years too old and belonged to someone who held a camera.

"Guess this will be the shortest episode ever.

Ready for me to call the medics and be done, terrorista? I don't think your God gets reception out here."

I willed the clay lump to fly at his handsome, black-haired head.

"What about footage?" the girl argued. "We don't have enough yet. My dad said this girl was promised to be gold. We're to get enough for a couple episodes, and she hasn't even made it to—"

I swallowed twice. "Keep going."

There was a pause.

"What'd the little fanatic say?"

I'd spoken in Amhebran. I tried again in English. "Keep going."

"OK, terrorista. If you say so. Yet we're not the ones lying in the dirt. You lead; we follow."

When I didn't move, the others found areas of shade and settled. Food wrappers rustled. The air grew pungent with garlic, salt, and cheese. Voices argued, then laughed. Happy Heathen. With their happy Heathen lives.

Somehow this was familiar. I'd suffered through this before. When? I focused harder, pushing against the pulse of pain that thinking brought on.

That evening last summer, when I'd been captured. I'd lain on Wolfe's grass after Diamond and her friends attacked me. Hurting and surrounded. Like now. I'd gotten away, hadn't I? How? I must remember. The image swam and went fuzzy.

Wolfe! He'd saved me. I needed Wolfe.

Wolfe? No, wait. Not him. God. Yes, I needed God. But also a human—someone with a pair of arms to carry me. Not Wolfe...but stronger arms.

A picture of an ashen-haired giant wafted under

my eyelids where everything was stained bright red. His name was Stone. Stone Bender. He'd do it. I think he'd offered once.

God? If you could tell Stone to carry me to water, I think that would be best...

~*~

I woke able to think clearly.

"Thank You," I breathed, recognizing this temporary miracle. My neck hairs tingled in the windless night.

I lifted my head, testing it. Only a little dizzy. The dark tent shapes at my back were silent except for some breathing. In front of me, the moon had cleared the ridge of nearby cliffs, inky obstacles below the star-specked sky.

A single star sputtered, brighter than the rest at the ridgeline. Flash. Flashflashflash.

I focused on the star.

Water, it said.

I sat up, the world spinning. *Gilead? Grandpa?* Back home they, my cousins, and I used flashlights to communicate in the dark from our sleeping porches. The flashes were a signal Grandpa had taught us. An Amhebran code, he'd said.

Sometimes my cousins and I used the code to signal unimportant stuff. Like "Good night." Or "Beware of squirrel." Grandpa used it only for important warnings, like when he sighted nighttime prowlers.

This code meant water. Which was odd. Usually the code was sent by the one requesting water. Was someone up on the ridge also dying of thirst? Another

Christian? That seemed unlikely. But how likely was it that a person who knew Amhebran could be up there anyway?

I slipped, soft-footed, in the direction of the distant cliffs. A half-dozen times I glanced back to where the tents sat. Had I shaken off Jessica, the unshakable girl who never allowed me to be more than two steps in front of her? Yet no human figure trailed after me. For now, I was safe.

Flash. Flash. Flashflashflash.

The cliffs loomed bigger, blocking out more stars. Except the one, which still sputtered. *Water*.

I touched the bluff's rough base, still warm from the day's solar rays. But now I could no longer see the flashes. I flung myself away from the crumbly wall and ran backward with my head tilted until my cockeyed bun pressed the base of my neck.

Flash. Flash.

I needed to respond. Should I yell? How far did sound carry out here? I stared into the darkness that hid the tents. If only I had brought my fire starter.

I cupped my hands. "Shalom?"

My whisper must have carried far enough. The on-off pattern stopped, becoming a steady, solid beam. It arced off the side of the cliff and fell onto a smallish boulder shaped like a potato, illuminating the ground below. Then the light cut off.

Breathing in shallow gasps, I crept until I touched the potato rock, a normal, dusty boulder up close. With a sigh of disappointment, I leaned against it and waited. Nothing happened—no flash, no sound of someone climbing down to meet me. I heaved myself up onto the rock and surveyed the expanse of cacti and dried-up prickle bushes from the top.

The flashes had lied. There was no water. No sympathetic, dehydrated believer suffering here.

My eyes hit on the leather pouch half wedged below the rock where I balanced. It was the kind Melody used to carry water. I leaped down, pried off the stopper, and jammed the opening against my lips.

Blissful liquid poured down my aching throat. I gasped between mouthfuls and coughed.

Thank you! Thank you, thank you.

My initial thirst satisfied, I perched on the rock and breathed deep. My arms hugged the water to my chest between swigs. The top of the cliff, so high up, remained inky and motionless.

With a jolt, I realized a light shone in the distance behind me. A far-off tent glowed from the campsite where I'd left my backpack.

I leaped up and drained the last drops of water. I had to return to the campsite for my belongings, and I had to hurry so I wouldn't lead anyone searching for me to my secret water supply…or to the person who'd saved my life, the one who knew Amhebran.

With a last glance up, I tossed the floppy leather at the rock and rabbited back through the spiky vegetation. At my approach, the tent's light switched off. My feet stepped only on the rocks and pieces of earth that muffled my steps. My pack lay ahead, a shapeless blob next to the boulder.

"Terrorista?"

It wasn't Jessica's whisper but a man's, but without its usual sneer.

I pulled out my metallic blanket, noisier than the nearby gentle snores and slow breathing. With a smug half smile, I turned my back to the camera whose glass circle gleamed in the moonlight.

12

Black, beady eyes stared into mine. Hungry, fearless eyes.

I lifted my head and flicked off the grasshopper. His brothers and sisters weren't intimidated by this and persisted to hop over and around me.

A dingy cloud, the same color as the ground, blocked the early dawn at the horizon. How much time did I have? Less than a minute? Thirty seconds? I plunged into my belongings and dragged out my tree tent.

I'd barely flung it up onto the boulder's edge, stuck the adjacent side to a nearby cactus, and climbed inside my primitive shelter when the swarm arrived. With a sudden, frantic hum, they smacked and crawled over the woven material.

Outside Jessica screamed, a single, high-pitched squeal.

"What is this?"

"Ouch! Geroff me!"

The panicked crew and their body guards shouted and swore. I remembered the bright tents' loose, unzipped openings. A mistake. Bugs must be covering their occupants like an ever-moving, second skin. A prickling dread ran over mine.

I pulled out my jar of bee repellant. My fingers fished out an acorn-sized, smoky, golden glob.

These weren't bees. And while I rubbed the jar's

oily contents over my hands, neck, and face, Gilead's voice growled at me to quit using up precious energy. I'd eaten nothing for a long time, and I should rest. But I slathered on the protective layer despite his raving. I had to, like instinct. The angry humming—the sound so similar to a buzz—demanded it.

One grasshopper, accompanied by three more, found their way in through my shelter's cracks. They sprang onto my legs and torso.

I dusted them off and picked up fist-sized lava rocks I'd slept among. I jammed them against the flaps of cloth, pinning my tent more firmly to the ground. Soon, no more intruders entered. I studied the couple dozen trapped inside. They were thistle-head sized, larger than the hoppers we had in Oregon, and funny looking. At the bottom of their tiny heads, their jaws stretched sharp and wider than normal.

I reached out to capture one, but it flew to the far corner and pressed against the tent's wall. And although they settled on my clothes and hair, they didn't get near my face or any of my exposed skin. The work of my repellant?

I cornered one, squished its head, and popped it into my mouth. My tongue rejected its flavor and crunch, but I swallowed. Between my family's garden, the honey from our hives, my mom's ability to call down birds, and my brother's hunting, there'd never been a need to eat creatures with exoskeletons. How did Melody Brae do this? Last summer she'd listed a hundred of her mom's recipes, fifty of them involving insects.

I chewed up another, this time removing its legs and wings first.

It's a squash seed. Only a dried squash seed. But I'd

never been able to lie. Not even to myself.

I captured, killed, and de-winged each trapped hopper and the few more that fought their way into my sloppy set up. Most entered from a small gap on the far side of the cactus. There was an opening there I couldn't reach without impaling myself on the inch-long, blond needles. I ate until my stomach stopped whining for sustenance, and then I began to make a pile for later. I'd smoke them when the swarm moved off. Smoke might mellow out the flavor.

My food source mound grew more impressive while I grew impatient, tying and retying the knot at my pack's opening between killing hoppers. I needed to hike south and reach my goal—Big Bend National Park—and from there get home. My fingers picked at the half-loose coil on my head, separating real hair from fake.

A low whimper outside my tent escalated as I untangled strands. By the time I flung the bun aside— throwing handfuls of pebbly sand on it to hide it—the whimpering set my teeth on edge as much as the patter and scrambling of grasshoppers.

I unstuck enough of my tent's opening to insert my head through. I squinted through the tiny bodies colliding with my face, ricocheting off. As if watching for me to appear, a hooded head poked out from a deluxe orange tent across from me. It yelled something.

"What?" How could the girl expect me to make out her words? The hood's material stretched tight over most of her face, including her mouth.

The material shifted. Lips appeared. "Are. You. Stung?"

Stung? Were the Heathen that clueless about bugs? These were hoppers. Not bees.

"You stung?" Jessica shouted again through the swarm. "No medics. Copter...no visibility...hang on...giving up?"

I retracted my head inside my enclosure to puzzle this out. She must think someone had been stung...and she was concerned about me?

I grimaced. Hardly. No, she only asked out of morbid curiosity, to find out how much the fanatic suffered.

Her other shouted fragments seemed to be about the medics not coming to help whoever was hurt because they couldn't see through the cloud. And she asked if I was giving up?

Nice try, Satan. You first.

Another human-sounding groan rose and fell, adding to the first person's whimpering. Great. Now I had to listen to two people moan in pain, as if they'd been stung. I'm from a family full of kids that keeps bees. I know being stung and how it sounds. I pinched a hopper and brought it up to my eyes, noting the sharp jaw. To bite with? Human flesh?

What freaky wilds had the Heathen brought me to? Well, they were the ones paying for it.

My brow furrowed as I fingered my jar of repellant, still three-quarters full. With a slow nod, I made my decision. The moment I peeked out my shelter's opening, the girl's hood emerged across from me.

"Here." I lobbed my jar at her. It was a bullseye toss and landed only a foot short, rolling the rest of the distance. The orange material she held around her neck jerked closed, as if I'd hurled her a wasps' nest.

A breath later Jessica reappeared.

"It's repellant!" Yelling hurt my throat. "Re-pellant! It'll keep you safe! Wear it on your skin! Your skin! Like me!"

Her face shifted inside her hood until a skeptical, almond eye fully appeared. My offered container began to disappear under the climbing bodies on the ground. I retracted with a shrug.

Fine. Don't believe me. Don't use it. Go ahead and get stung or bit.

I spent the rest of the day memorizing Governor Ruth's message from the sweat-marked paper and trying to pray over the hum, whimpers, and groans. As the gloom deepened for night, I crammed the dead hoppers into the spaces of my pack so I had more room to sleep. I figured even if I discovered more appetizing food sources and ended up not eating them, they'd cushion my head tonight.

Shaboom. Something larger than a hopper shook my shelter. I grabbed the woven material to keep it in place as the tent's sides shivered from another blow.

Rocks? Was someone chucking rocks at me? I picked up my own lava stone weapon and kneeled at the opening.

Brown flecks sprang and ricocheted. Across from me, the orange tent's opening stayed tight shut. But next to my own flap laid my returned bee repellant jar. And a water bottle. It was heavy, filled to the bottleneck with clear liquid.

13

On the fourth night of the grasshopper siege, I awoke to low groans. Only groans—no hum. I blinked in the brightness of the locust-free moonlight and jumped up, hooking my fur sleeve on the cactus in my eagerness.

Never would I pitch my tent against a cactus again. I scrambled out of my tent. A familiar rhythmic beating drew my eyes to the starry sky. Stretching my spine, I watched the helicopter clear the distant cliffs and make its way over.

That flying machine represented everything I hated about pagans, including their lies, tricks, and confidence in stupid technology. If only Wolfe were here with his power-killing EMPs.

I whipped my collapsed tent up and down in the dry air, clearing it of dust and debris. A few grasshopper carcasses flew up and landed near my feet. With an eye on the sky, I thrust one in my mouth and chewed, my teeth gnashing in disgust and anger.

I sensed the camera before I saw it. The smugly handsome cameraman grinned at my snack and gestured. *Keep eating. Don't let me stop you.* No doubt he was pumped he could show the Heathen world proof. Christians do eat bugs.

"Over here!" Jessica stepped around from the other side of the boulder where I poised, frozen. She waved like an idiot at the helicopter, as if it'd miss us in this barren landscape.

I hiked a couple of feet away to take refuge in the midst of an evil-looking cacti cluster. Cacti and bare sticks were the only vegetation in sight. Even with only the moon's illumination, I could tell the green tufts from four days ago made the wasteland look like paradise, compared to what it was now.

"Here! We're over here!" Jessica wormed her way to me through the tangle of cacti. She used her small frame to her advantage. It also increased her annoyingness tenfold.

"What was in that lotion you gave me, fanatic? And how'd you know you'd need it here in Texas?"

I shoved my balled-up tent into my bag, no doubt crushing my food supply. Dust and unnatural wind blew into my eyeballs as the vehicle touched down.

"Did you get stung? Hey, answer me. Did you?"

I glared up. "Did you?"

"One sting. Hurts. But I've had worse."

A group of harassed workers in maroon uniforms loaded the two men—the wider ones I called "guards"—onto flat boards. They trooped back to the helicopter.

I craned my neck. The guards' skin seemed darker in the limited light, but not that swollen. Not bad enough for the full-grown men to whimper worse than my little cousin, Jovie, after she rolls out of her hammock.

Jessica also focused on the medics but still held her typical, tense stance. Her hand nearest me clenched and unclenched. She'd been stung? The girl was either a liar or tougher than these men.

A small, smirking figure looped his way to us

through the cacti. He handed the girl her camera.

She accepted. "Close call. Looks like you escaped with your face still pretty."

He poked a black cattail object on a pole at me. "Stay, terrorista. It won't bite if you don't. Speak into the microphone and answer this. Six days down...eight to go. So does your God reward faith with fast legs?"

Jessica rubbed her bare forearm, which gleamed with the oily film of repellant. "No. He only provides lotion."

~*~

Rocky cliffs converged on either side as I trudged south. My eyes scanned their flat tops. So far there was no sign of whoever gifted me the water pouch days ago. I hadn't made anymore nighttime trips to the bluff with the potato rock at its base because of the swarms...and also because water bottles had shown up every morning and night at my tent's entrance.

Yet I didn't hold my breath for any more water bottles from the crew. The unspoken trade—repellant for water—had ended with the last grasshopper.

The new cliffs provided shade but made the hiking treacherous with all the scattered boulders and ankle-twisting rubble underfoot. Plus, there were snakes. Twice I spotted coiled bodies in hollows under piles.

As I skirted another rattler, the edge of a cloudbank covered the sun. Without its warm rays, the land grew duller and uglier.

"What's that over there?" The remaining guard pointed a thick finger. Cameras swiveled.

Beyond his nail, a bright color shimmered from

the distant dust at ground level. My legs tried to hurry but only stumbled to the bank of a shallow, dried up riverbed. At its very bottom lay a helicopter-sized pool.

I leaned over the red, scummy water speckled with dead locusts. My eyes darted to the others who'd remained with me. Did they see color as well? Or was I having some sort of hallucination? Was I imagining red?

"Thirsty, terrorista?" The cameraman winked.

In that moment, I understood the reason I was thirsty and stared at filthy, bright water. Undrinkable water was part of my Christian survival struggle. And the Heathen had discovered enough about the Bible to dye the water red. Water turned to blood. Hordes of bugs. These were the Egyptian plagues.

The godless toyed with me and mocked God through my thirst and my struggles. The producers of *Fanatic Surviving* must have thought themselves clever in creating these scenarios.

The guard stepped between me and the cameraman who persisted in calling me a terrorist. My need to slam something must have shown because the guard cracked his knuckles in anticipation. I tamped down my outburst and shoved around him, striding southward. Even though I could drink this water if I boiled it, I wouldn't.

Jokes on you, Fanatic Surviving.

"How does she keep going without drinking? For days and days? Six days? It's...it's impossible."

The corners of my lips twitched up. At last I'd wiped the smirk off the handsome face.

Jessica matched my stride, keeping out of striking distance. Because I was a dangerous Christian. Yet a wave of discomfort—guilt?—flickered over her face.

Aha. So she'd broken the rules by passing me those water bottles and hadn't told the others.

I toe-flicked a tan clump into her path. That got her attention. My eyes held her almond ones for two steps. *I could tell them. What you did.*

I wouldn't. How would tattling on her help me? But I let her worry.

My satisfaction faded at the same time my legs began to drag like half-dead tree trunks. I veered and dropped into the empty riverbed I'd been following. I continued to clump south over the parched, cracked ground.

Would this dried mud path lead to more water? Liquid, at one time, had formed this bed and was responsible for its baked-in snakeskin pattern. There could be another pool.

By midday my head ached. There was no water...there wouldn't be...and it'd been dumb to leave the cruddy puddle behind without collecting any of it. I should go back.

My dehydrated body lumbered onward.

To the northeast behind me, the horizon grew dark and fuzzy with the promise of rain. But the clouds seemed stuck at the hills, no doubt releasing their water too far away to help me. Thunder rumbled.

The cameraman let out a sudden burst of laughter. "Tired of hoppers? Yum, yum. Ratones."

A couple rodents—but not rats—scuttled up the crumbling sides of the dried riverbed to my right. One paused on its oversized legs to nibble a flat oval cactus. Then it disappeared.

I licked my cracked lips and clambered on all fours up to higher ground after the creatures. Grass tufts grew near the cactus the rodent had gnawed. That meant we'd come further south than the swarms.

I wet my lips again. Did I have enough strength left in me to do what I needed to do? I shut my lids and concentrated through the pounding in my skull.

Lord? Do I?

I could feel a million eyes watching me.

Ignoring the cameras, I found two dead sticks and used them to trap and rip three oval sections off the cactus plant. The thorns of this kind weren't as big as the ones I'd stretched my tent over. And if animals could eat this type of cactus, I'd be suicidal not to try.

"Move back from her, out of my shot, Jessica," the cameraman ordered. "Here. Take the boom."

The black cattail object on a pole swung near my cheek. I knocked it away and carried on, scraping the thorns from my cactus piece with a sharp rock. I panted as I worked. My hands shook with the effort.

"My producer likes it when you fanatics explain what you're doing. It makes you more interesting to the viewers."

I shrugged my backpack onto a tuft and fished out my fire starter. Then I slid down the slope, back into the dry bed, clutching it and the smooth, green, hopefully edible plant. But I nodded once at his bluntness. He didn't pretend I struggled for anything greater than Heathen enjoyment. Harsh but honest.

In the dusty basin, my steel scraped flint twice. Its sparks ignited the dead grass pile. I glanced up through the smoke puffs. "Then tell your producer to come out here himself to do this survival stuff. He can chat it up all he wants and explain how he stays alive."

He chuckled. His laugh held a nicer tone than usual.

Crouching, I toasted my grasshopper cache in

batches on the hot rocks balanced in my tiny fire. The dry brush burned up as if it were soaked in tree sap, but the cactus flesh gave me liquid energy to keep adding sticks and grass. I gulped it down while I worked.

"Secret family recipe, terrorista?"

Sprawled on the bank at the top of the slope next to my stuff, both crewmembers had set their cameras and the cattail boom aside to eat their wrapped food bars.

The lamebrain forgot I'm from Oregon, a place with too many resources for my family to resort to eating insects. And no cacti. Although the cactus flesh wasn't terrible. It had a green bean flavor. But it was so slimy. Yet slime meant water.

The remaining guard made an irritated movement next to me. Was it my fire that bothered him? My unappetizing meal? Or simply my presence? Or maybe that I did so well in Texas when his guard pals had to be stretched out on boards and helicoptered away?

The smell of his nervous sweat reached my nostrils through the smoke.

I paused in my chewing. Did he have to sit so close? What did he think I could do with this small fire, turn it into a weapon?

I glanced at the gloomy cliffs on either side and shivered in the warm, static air. I spat my last bite of chewed cactus into the ash. My stomach knotted. Perhaps eating that cactus slime hadn't been so wise.

Vibrations shivered up from the dry dust into my soles. I glanced around and saw nothing suspicious. Yet the sound of a thousand enemies charged at me with an echoing, death roar. At the roar's heels came the command from heaven.

Stand.

I obeyed an instant before the wall of brown water rounded the bend. Higher than the banks and my head, the water rushed at me, led by a crest with sticks and debris reaching out like spears.

My feet wouldn't move, only my arms. They raised up, like a kid asking to be lifted.

Father—

The lethal wall struck.

14

I smacked the ground, flew up, and spun. I couldn't find my way to air through the liquid mud. My lungs and stomach seemed to burst with the stuff as something solid jabbed into my side. The object raked my skin—like another flood victim clinging to me by its fingernails for help. But that sharp pain didn't compare to the burning in my chest.

With my next toss and roll, brightness flashed behind my lids. For an instant, I opened my eyes to the sky and my mouth to oxygen. I sucked in a lungful of air before being tugged back down under the brown sludge. I tried to keep track of which way was up. Up was brighter.

As the violent flow swept me along, I flailed and kicked like Gilead taught me last summer. My effort was enough to bring me vertical so my head broke the surface every few seconds. But my body was used up. I couldn't keep fighting. And up ahead were the rocks.

Rocks. An understatement. They weren't just clumsy boulders in my path but the roughhewn cliff itself. I was far enough back from the raging flood's spearhead that I saw the wall of water crash against the vertical stone with an earth-shattering blast. And when the sky-reaching splash came back down, it forced its way into a jagged hole at the cliff's base, where it was sucked down and out of sight...to where? An underground canyon? An abyss?

I was going to strike the cliff, too. At the last moment, I cranked myself around so my spine and the back of my skull hit the rock instead of my face.

Bright lights popped. Darkness followed, joined by a relaxing haze. My slack legs became trapped in the flow's power and pulled behind me, banging the edge of the rock. Why fight it? If only the cliff would let me rest once it swallowed me...that would be a relief. *Let me rest.*

A sharp pain under my ribs jolted me. What? What was I doing? *Fight, Dove, fight!* Panic zinged through each water-logged cell in my body. My legs were trapped in the hole but only my legs. My torso stayed bent, pinned against the cliff that hurt me, crushing my sore ribs. My arms scrambled to hold on to the slippery rock.

Something new squeezed under my struggling arms. A bar locked around my chest, and my oxygen escaped in a whoosh. The bar was strong. It fought against the torrent, pulling my body away from the vertical rock I hugged, away from the sucking hole.

My legs scraped sharpness again. Then my feet and my head cleared the water. I dragged in air between sputters. The roar of the flood faded a little, replaced by my coughs and the faint, gritty crunch of footsteps. Nothing tugged now, but my body was carried along.

I opened my eyes to a cloudy sky. I squinted up at the dripping, familiar, ash-brown beard.

"Stone?"

15

After my one croaked word, neither Stone Bender nor I spoke. I was too busy trying to breathe and choke up the gallons I'd inhaled. Before I finished, he halted and slid me onto the ground. His hands positioned my head on a tuft of dried grass, and he nodded as if satisfied.

My lips moved, tried to form words. Questions. Commands.

How'd you know I was here? How'd you get here? Don't go! Don't leave me!

But he abandoned me and sprinted for the cliff—the dry side away from the brown river overflowing its banks. His gaze connected with mine and then flickered away.

Don't go, Stone!

He grabbed a hidden handhold in the sheer rock and flew like a spider up the outcropping. Within seconds he rounded a protrusion in the face and vanished. My hand that had reached after him flopped back onto the gravelly sand. It weighed a thousand pounds. How had I ever managed to lift it before?

I wiggled my other heavy limbs, testing them. The sodden wet fur I wore seemed to make my extremities even more unwieldly. But how was my body not mangled or broken? Only scraped and exhausted? Fur couldn't have protected me that much.

God. It was You, God. Thank You. For the miracle.

Was Stone a miracle, too? Had he rescued me, or had I dreamed it?

I dragged myself to my knees and half-crawled over to where he had begun his climb. The vertical wall was vacant. Only darker, wet smudges remained as evidence he'd been real.

I stared at those shiny spots his feet and body had made. Stone couldn't be here in Texas. The idea was impossible. He had left his brother, Reed, over a week ago on Mount Jefferson. He would have made it to his home on Mount Washington before I'd even reached Governor Ruth. And all that happened a million miles away in Oregon.

"Stone!" My plea came out in a throaty rasp.

Someone answered me. It wasn't the person I wanted, and the response came from the opposite direction of the cliff. "Oh. You're not drowned?"

Jessica bounded toward me. Everything about her was dry—including my backpack dangling from her outstretched hand. She threw it onto a low boulder nearby and leveled her camera. The cattail boom's pole seesawed under her armpit. "Sit. While you dry off, tell how you did it. Lobo says hundreds of people each year die in these flashfloods, where it rains far away in the mountains, and all the water rushes into the low spots in the desert. So how did you survive?"

I hadn't been paying attention to names this week. But it seemed I'd heard the word *lobo* a lot. Was Lobo the small, dark cameraman? My heavy shoulders lifted in a shrug.

Her camera inched closer. "Was it because you're a strong swimmer? Is that something your God demands of you people, the skill to survive floods? In your religion, your God sends floods to kill people He doesn't like, right?"

I collapsed on the rock with a wet noise and gritted my teeth. *Go away.*

Her arrival prevented me from getting to Stone. If she went away, I could climb after him, find him and talk to him.

Part of me knew this was both dumb and unfair. I had no strength. I'd fall if I tried to climb the cliff right now. But my helplessness, my frustration, bubbled into words.

"You call this...*Fanatic Surviving*, yeah? And you base each of my failures on how weak my God is. And on my lack of faith in Him?"

I waited for her nod and then continued. "OK, then. Let me ask you a question. Do you have brains?"

She jerked up from her camera in surprise.

"I'll take that as a yes. And since you claim to have brains, it seems like you should be able to use them to answer your own question. How did I survive? And maybe you're, in fact, smart enough to realize you're seeing only victories here with me instead of failures. I'm asking you—for real. C'mon. How did I survive? Say it! Say it! How?"

The camera lowered. "Because of...your...God?" she whispered. Her response was another secret between her and me, like the water bottles. Not for the camera or the television-watching nonbelievers.

I slumped over my wet knees. My outburst had zapped my ability to move, and if she'd only go away, I'd sleep right here on this flat rock. Perhaps I'd shocked and insulted her enough that she would walk away and go bug someone else like the cameraman, Lobo. And then I wouldn't have to go after Stone. He'd return when he saw I was alone.

She leaned her hip against my rock. Her choice to move closer didn't fool me, though. Under her purple shirt, her lean body stayed tight and ready to react. "I'd wondered why they chose you, Pickett. For *Fanatic Surviving*. I mean, I knew you had connections. But now I get it. You're exactly what a Christian fanatic should be. You always looked the part. But now you sound like one too—do you know how delusional you sound? How crazy?" She slipped into a mutter. "And you're making me say crazy things, too."

I shrugged. Then sniffed. Why was there smoke in the air? I'd heard thunder earlier. Had lightning struck something flammable in this desert?

The camera leveled again. "Those furs look heavy, Pickett. Why do you choose to wear them?"

I felt my lip curl. "Not to be rude, but go away— far out of my sight. Come back tonight when it's dark. I'll be here. I won't run. You have my word."

"Not to be rude, fanatic, but I don't believe you. Plus, Lobo and his camera will be catching up to us here any minute. I let him know I was going to search next to the riverbed. He was waiting for the medics to finish before following."

Medics?

I'd forgotten I hadn't been alone in the dry riverbed when the flash flood ambushed me. I bit my lip, watching the distant helicopter rise up into the low cloud cover and head north. I waited until the helicopter's *chop, chop, chop* died out. "Did...did the guard guy...did he—"

"No. Not yet at least. Only knocked unconscious. He got caught on a pile of dead sticks at the bank right away. Lobo was able to get to him and keep his head above the water until medics arrived. They were planning to call in a search for your body, but no need I guess."

I moved to the edge of the river that flowed with less rage now. Water still swirled and sucked into the hole at the cliff's base.

The message! Had it been ripped away?

I tumbled to my knee as if hit. My fingers probed inside my sock until they closed upon the folded paper plastered against my ankle.

I collapsed onto my rear and let out my shaky breath. The message felt whole, the edges square. I wouldn't remove it now, though, to make sure. The wet paper might rip in my hands, and I wasn't alone.

I leaned over and scooped some dingy water into my bottle to filter and clean later when I was thirsty. Odd to think I'd ever crave water again. I pretended to watch the murky flow, but my eyes kept darting up at a certain cliff. Still nothing...no one appeared.

The cameraman, Lobo, trudged into view with his wet clothes stuck to him, looking almost as worn as I felt. The camera girl skittered over the rocks to meet him, and they retraced some of his steps, pausing behind a spiky, chest-high bush to converse in low voices. The water's noise level had fallen. Most words reached my ears.

"Lightning?"

"The lightning started a fire...they said it shouldn't catch us."

"—but wait for how long?"

"I'm OK with it. You?"

"If she's not a threat then—"

"—wait for a guard or..."

I rose and tossed a rock into the brown depths.

Kerplunk. "If you're trying to be secretive, you need to move yourselves farther away. And we'll keep moving south tonight. There's no point in waiting until morning for the helicopter to bring in someone else to guard you. You don't need a guard."

Lobo crossed his arms. He picked his way over to me. "It's not your choice, terrorista. It's ours. Jessica's. She gets to decide this."

She stared north, looked at me, and then faced south. "She could have hurt me a bunch of times the last few days. And she hasn't. No guard—if you're good with that, Lobo?"

He laughed—that ugly, hard laugh—and pushed his knuckles into the insides of his biceps the way Gilead did to intimidate. "I'm fine without one. I was never afraid of her. But, terrorista, remember that I'm small but way strong and a light sleeper."

My own hand waved away his warning and then pointed northeast. "About this lightning fire you say is burning over there. I don't know this land. Texas." I spat the name like it was a bitter bug. "You trust the information you received? That the fire won't reach us? Because I think we should assume it will and keep moving."

"It'll burn out when it hits the part of the land that the hoppers picked clean. There's nothing much there to burn."

"Hmph!"

Lobo sneered at my doubt. "Our team would pull us out right now if they thought there was a chance we'd get surrounded by a wildfire. They wouldn't risk our lives."

"Our lives" meant the camera crew's lives. Not mine. Because that was what those watching *Fanatic*

Surviving wanted to see. The Christian fanatic, who'd escaped stinging insects, week-long dehydration, and a flash-flood, being caught in a raging wildfire. And not surviving.

16

I sprawled on the desert floor. The sleep sounds from the others were loud. My mouth fell open, and I blinked. I blinked again, this time longer. Too long.

I forced my scratchy lids to open again and stared into the utter blackness of the night. Tonight, clouds or smog veiled the stars, so it was easy to find the one that sputtered low in the sky.

Flashflashflash.

With my fire starter in my grasp, I sneaked away from the tents and faced Stone's Amhebran signal. I paused to stretch and sniff. Lobo had been right. The lightning fire had burned out. Only a trace of smoke still hung in the air.

Since clouds covered the moon too, I hiked with extra caution, but finally I made it to the cliff's base. Before I even had a chance to ignite the dried branch I'd brought along to signal a reply, the light arced off the cliff like before. This time it fell to illuminate a tall cactus with pudgy arms near its bottom. A saguaro, Lobo had called this kind of cactus.

The same leather pouch as last time balanced low on the saguaro's crooked extremity. No human giant waited for me next to it. Disappointment cut me so deep I hunched over, hugging myself. Where was he? Why hadn't he come to meet me?

"Stone," I whispered. "Stone! I'm here!"

I straightened and dropped my arms. OK. So Stone wasn't going to climb down to meet me. Fine. It's not like he would be able to do anything helpful tonight or tomorrow or the next day. I was supposed to be surviving alone on my trek south.

My arms curled back around my waist. I couldn't lie. Believing I would see him tonight had kept me walking the last few painful hours. What a relief it would have been to have had a friend—or at least another Christian—within sight when surrounded by enemies in this hostile, alien land.

The pouch's strap scraped and tangled on the long needles until I unhooked it with a final yank. I threw my head back and filled my mouth with the liquid I didn't need. Water was something I'd had plenty of today.

I choked and spat out my mouthful.

The bitter taste twinged my taste buds. I spat again, trying to get rid of every nasty drop. Inside my mouth, my tongue and cheeks prickled.

I sniffed the water container. My nose picked up on an odd scent, though subtle. It tasted much worse than it smelled. What was wrong with this water?

Judging by the changes inside my mouth, something toxic had been mixed in. Something that if I'd swallowed it, would have done some serious damage. Perhaps it would've knocked me out cold...or killed me.

I emptied the contents into the dust and flung the leather into the darkness.

Everything was silent. So still—a heavy, expectant stillness.

I chewed my tongue and shuddered. The night was so black. With another shiver, I picked my way back toward my campsite. My tongue and cheeks were numb but not blistered or anything worse.

Conflicting assumptions blossomed, crowding my brain so I had a difficult time focusing on where to tread.

I'd been wrong. The water giver wasn't Stone. Unless Stone wanted to poison me...which seemed not only unlikely, since he'd saved me from drowning, but way too vengeful for him. Poison was too dramatic a weapon. Sure, I'd rejected him last September. But even if I'd hurt his feelings, he hadn't become my enemy. I'd seen at least that much in his dripping wet face. And whoever this was, this water giver, this person was out to hurt me.

But that made no sense either. Why give me clean, drinkable water a week ago when I would have died without it? If this person wanted me dead—or not to finish my journey—then leaving me alone days ago and letting dehydration take its toll would have been easier. Why give me water at all? Just to keep me alive until he or she could then poison me?

My next thought made me halt and reface the cliff. Where was Stone tonight during all the light flashing and water giving? Did he know about the water giver? He couldn't know, or he'd have stopped the person. Was Stone in trouble? Should I flash him the Amhebran message for danger?

I turned, and a shaft of light nailed me in the retinas. "Where've you been, terrorista?"

I ducked out of Lobo's flashlight beam. He kneeled at the opening of his green tent, which I'd almost collided with in my distracted walking.

"Tell me. Explain. What do you search for out there?" The beam swung out at the prickly plants and dust.

Already my mouth's numbness began to wear off. But I didn't speak. Pinching my tongue between my thumb and forefinger, I laid down and crossed my arms to wait. When Lobo gave up and fell asleep, I would signal "danger" to Stone. I only needed to stay awake.

~*~

My eyelids opened with a jerk. Oh no. I'd made a huge mistake—I'd slept too deep. My lungs contracted against the thick air. I finished coughing, then shoved my blanket and bottle into my bag, scattering hoppers. "Get up! Get up!"

Zippers buzzed and fabric rustled. Heads appeared, but veiled in the smoky, early dawn light, so I couldn't make out their expressions.

"The fire! From the lightning. It's burning close." The effects of the bad water had worn off, so my shout was coherent. Why weren't there any sounds of frenzied departure?

"Impossible. It was out." Lobo yawned and then leaned out to survey me. His face loomed, suspicious. "How do you know?"

Because I'm not an idiot.

I ripped a section of the tent's pole frame out of Jessica's hand.

"Hey!"

I chucked the plastic piece as far as I could throw. "No time to pack up. Leave the tent. Grab your food and water."

"And cameras." Lobo must have decided to use

his brain cells. "She's not playing, Jesse. Grab your shoes and camera and we *vamanos*!"

"But Daddy gave me my tent for—"

I threw her boot at her. "You can have mine, a gift from my whole family. Put on your shoes. C'mon." Flickers of orange stayed out of sight, but the wisps of ash beginning to fall warned me they were close.

~*~

I led back to where we'd ditched the riverbed last night. Waves of unnatural air licked my cheeks. Stomping in my footsteps, the crew offered suggestions to what level of suicidal I'd become.

With a wheeze of thankfulness, I located the trickle of brown water I backtracked for. It rested lower than I hoped in its riverbed that started back up from an underground water channel.

"You're...still taking us...the wrong direction—" A messy splash behind me interrupted Jessica's panted observation.

I reached backward. My hand touched the warmth of her bare forearm and yanked her up onto dry ground. I ignored her gasp. "Quit messing with your camera and pay attention to where you step. Falling slows us down. I know what I'm doing."

This was a decent plan...wasn't it? If I stayed by the riverbed and jumped into these few inches of water, the liquid would save us from being burned if the fire caught up. Wouldn't it? I stole the idea from that hunter on Mount Washington whose charred electronic I'd discovered last summer. Except he'd died in that fire so...

Lobo chuckled. "Not quite enough agua for that, terrorista."

I swung around. "You want to lead?"

"Always. But I'm not the t—"

"Stop calling me a terrorist. Is anyone going to complain if we ditch the water and head for those far cliffs?"

Lobo fell into step beside me. "That's what I'd do. If I was in charge. Which I'm not."

I paused and fished my plastic bottle from my backpack. Who knew if I'd have another chance to gather water today? "Call first on your radio. Call your people and make sure we're still safe, that the fire isn't catching us if we go more west."

"But you see, terrorista—"

"My name is Dove."

"Well, you see, Dove, I am in charge of that." He raised his wrist with the electronic attached. "I make the decision when to call."

"Call 'em, Lobo." Jessica flopped down on the bank and wiped her damp face on her shirtfront.

He saluted and wandered a few yards away. When he returned, I didn't cut his explanation short, although I'd overheard his conversation.

He fiddled, rebuckling a strap that didn't need fixing. "Apparently, the aircrew, they...er...said they weren't aware of a blaze so far this direction. The one from yesterday burned itself out, and oh, they—uh—the fire watch thinks lightning must have struck again during the night. And that this is a fresh fire. But we're safe. The wind plus the geography...well, they say this one will burn out too before it reaches farther south."

"Hmph!"

Jessica put my own disbelief into words. "More

lightning started this one? I didn't hear more lightning or see a flash. Wouldn't it have awakened us? At least one of us would have noticed."

Lobo stopped fidgeting. "We can stand here scratching our heads, or we can do something productive. That is, assuming the fanatic wants to keep going?"

I jerked my thumb at the southwest cliffs.

He grinned. "Following you, terr—Dove."

For hours, I picked through the growing amount of rubble piles at the base of the cliffs. My neck muscles burned from craning my head back to locate a logical spot to ascend and escape the distant but pursuing fire. With the helicopter stirring up debris and clogging my ears with its noise, I hunted through the opaque haze with dull senses.

Why did this new fire burn? No. Scratch that. The water-stained message from Ruth rubbed against my ankle with each step, a reminder that addressed the *why*. I was a messenger, so Satan hunted me. He didn't want my brother, or any other bloodthirsty Oregonian, to find out about the message that it was God's will for peace.

No, the real question was—*how* had Satan lit the fire?

Lightning hadn't flashed during the night. Even Jessica realized that. And at the time of my midnight hike to the Amhebran coder, I hadn't smelled much smoke. Which meant the northern fire had burned out, and this was a new blaze.

I sighed at the only explanation remaining. Satan had set this morning's fire using a human. A real, living, person who—at least early this morning—had roamed this desert with a desire to do evil. An arsonist had created the fire.

The image of a burning, tumbledown shack flared up before my squinted eyes. Reed smiled down from his lookout, a mossy precipice jutting from the evergreens. He used moss to scrub the lighter fluid off his palms.

No. I swiped the evil depiction away.

Now a stranger on a bicycle circled my family's maples with his gas can. My dad, Jonah Strong, stepped out of a fir's shadows and approached him. The rider reached into his jacket pocket. His hand emerged clenched around—not a lighter—but a weapon. There was a click, then...

I flopped onto a slanted boulder surrounded by flammable, dry stuff. A bird in a nest. My middle ached with a knot that my knuckles, pressing into my furs, couldn't knead away. Jessica lowered her camera and sank next to me, too worn to jerk away when her elbow brushed mine.

Had her people—the people in the helicopter—lit the fire? They'd claimed no knowledge of it before Lobo called. But could they be as brainless as they acted? They alone had the best motive besides hate. What would be more awesome, in their minds, than me running from a wildfire? Heathen television watchers would cheer.

But they'd already pulled out three of their guards because of injuries. Wouldn't they need to be more careful with the remaining camera crew, Jessica and Lobo?

If it wasn't the *Fanatic Surviving* people, then the arsonist would be the same stranger who'd tried to poison me last night. But why use fire? That stranger would have had the perfect opportunity to attack me last night when I was alone. Why choose this sloppy, drawn-out, fire route? I shook my head and tried to shoo away the obvious third option.

Stone?

No. He could not be a possible suspect. If Stone was here in Texas—and I was starting to wonder if I'd hallucinated him—then he wouldn't have lit a fire to hurt me. He wouldn't hurt me.

Even though he was experienced with fire, like his brother Reed? Stone was the same person who set fire to his hometown mountain last year and routed a group of men into its inferno. So why would he mind burning some sand dunes and a couple more people?

Lobo reappeared in the haze from his further wandering. He shook his water bottle at us. "No time for siestas. We have to move."

"Radio 'em again first, Lobo."

He obeyed Jessica, his quick questions and replies drowned out by the helicopter passing overhead. The girl next to me pulled out her contoured water bottle that fit her grasp. My dry throat spasmed with each of Jessica's satisfying gulps.

I had water. But with zero time to clean it, mine was still murky and brown.

Lobo refaced us. "The wind's not helping us. The wildfire's front is gaining, but they say we're still safe. It's our call—and yours." He nodded at me.

I crossed my arms. "Keep going. But we get to higher ground."

I waited for their arguments for giving up, but both nodded.

We stumbled forward faster. My eyes stayed glued to the cliff on my right, zigzagging the choppy surface, searching for a route up to its top that stayed hidden by the smoke screen. Jessica grabbed onto my pack with a jerk while rock debris echoed behind us. Lobo didn't speak either when she muttered something about a broken ankle. He continued to study the cliff converging on our left.

I stopped so abruptly that Jessica shoved against me. "Watch it, Pickett!"

To my right, flanked by two ancient, bird-pecked saguaros, a section of vertical wall formed a definite slope, almost an animal trail. I tried the slope, only to drop down, my muscles quivering with exhaustion. But this had to be our escape route. Unlike some other potentials I'd sighted, this way had decent footholds farther up where the face got vertical again. This was our best bet.

I will be your strength.

I wasn't thirsty anymore. My knees didn't tremble.

"I found a way up. Hurry up if you're coming with me." I stepped back onto the slope, balanced on the balls of my feet, hugged the rough rock face, and skittered ten feet up the first part of the six-inch wide path.

Lobo copied me. He was an efficient but suspicious climber, not choosing most of the holds I used. Was he wary I was setting him up to fall? Jessica was about as good at climbing as Melody. Blood dripped from a cut on her chin before she'd cleared the cacti.

"This..." Lobo mopped the sweat from his brow after heaving her up, "is going to be great fun. Give me your camera, Jesse."

"No."

I left them squabbling about who should film our climb and who needed both hands free. I eased my shoes off the skinny path and free climbed up another fifteen feet. Savage wind struck me the same moment orange broke through the haze on the ground.

I gripped the rock harder, hands slippery with sweat. I saw now what I hadn't been able to glimpse from further down. A line of flame chewed the ground while moving for the cliffs and out to the far horizon. Certain sections rose in flickering walls. Other areas smoldered black, as if the land was burned-out ash. Smoke billowed up from everywhere the fire touched. My blonde strands slapped my face in gusts, and an eerie whistling rose and fell.

"Pickett? You up there? Don't you go tumbling off without me getting it on camera!"

I searched the rock face that stretched higher until disappearing in the smoke. It wouldn't be a terrible climb alone.

"Pickett!"

Gritting my teeth, I skittered down to where the others waited.

I led the group back up, following the goat trail or whatever path this was. No hoofprints or droppings revealed what creatures traveled this way, but the going was too obvious for it not to be a path. The bright blob of the obscured sun disappeared over the ridge. Would it be possible to reach the top by night? Climbing in the darkness wouldn't be safe, at least not for them.

Jessica seemed to echo my thoughts.

"Safe? This is not any type of safe." Her almond-shaped, bloodshot eyes glared out over the flames far below. A dried smear of blood still streaked her chin "Call 'em Lobo. Tell them they're picking me up. I'm not dying for this."

I pressed my free forearm against the leap of panic in my gut. She was quitting?

Yet hadn't that been what I wanted from the beginning? To be rid of these people? Her?

Yes. No...

Sky alive, I needed her! Take away Jessica, and I remained with one camera person. Would *Fanatic Surviving* let me continue with only one? And would Lobo keep going if it was just him and me?

As Lobo finished the call for Jessica's airlift out, he caught me staring. He frowned. "They say there's a flat spot where they can land at the top of this ridge. The chopper will be waiting there. But we have to reach it in the next hour, before it gets much darker and the smoke any thicker...or this wind any worse."

I leaned down to hear him through the approaching helicopter and scream of the wind. He pointed at the smoke screen, hundreds of feet up and in the opposite direction of the sloping creature trail we followed.

Jessica glared at him. "Why can't they just drop a rope?

Lobo retorted something about safety and protocol with different rescue groups. Their voices spilled around me, but I forgot everything but climbing and holding tight. I jammed my toes onto a four-inch ledge, hugged the wall, and seized Jessica's satchel when Lobo shouted at me.

An eerie, pulsating brightness grew at our backs, and I broke out in sweat from warmth that wasn't just from climbing. I jerked upright at the sudden sound of a helicopter overhead.

"I'll kill them!" Jessica threatened.

Twinkling its lights in farewell, Jessica's rescue

vehicle faded into the vast sky. I dropped back onto the crumbly, three-foot long lip next to her and peered into the flames that reached the base of our bluff.

Lobo landed on the other side of me. "The crew's circling, finding a better spot to reach us! Don't worry, Jesse! They're coming back."

I couldn't tell from Lobo's hearty tone if he lied.

Jessica smacked my sleeve and said something I couldn't hear over the wail of the wind. Then she gestured up. Overhead, a wider chunk of rock jutted over us like an awning—an easy enough obstacle for me to get over. But it was an impossible barrier for this nonbeliever whose lean muscles couldn't get her up a simple, sloping path. Could Lobo handle an undercut climb like this? He was a decent climber for someone who wasn't a tree dweller.

"The fire won't reach us! We're too high!" He shouted confidently. For sure he was lying. "It'll hit the cliff and die...you watch! Fire don't burn just rock! It'll need fuel. You're safe, Jesse. Don't fear. Fire don't burn rock."

The saguaros at the foot of the slope began to blacken. In a blink, the flames shot up, creating an almost vertical, glowing zigzag that skipped and popped. It was as if the fire seared our exact path up the cliff.

It had. The wildfire was following our trail.

My breath hitched in my throat. I'd made a huge mistake. I shouldn't have chosen this route, shouldn't have climbed this welcoming slope that had also invited dirt to settle and vegetation to sprout up.

I didn't have to peer down into the smoke billows to see all the flammable, tufty things we'd passed that were starting to ignite and crackle. I remembered. I'd used them as hand and footholds the last couple of hours.

Choosing to climb any other spot of the cliff would have been safer, at least for the others. Myself, I wasn't stuck on this ledge—not like they were. I was a tree dweller. A girl who could outclimb the flames.

As I located my first foothold to propel myself up to the jutting rock above my head, I remembered something else. The realization jarred me like a kick in the forehead.

I was the only one here who had accepted Christ's salvation, the only one not damned to an eternity in Hell with forever separation from God. Which meant I was the only one ready to die. These nonbelievers weren't ready to face God, I was, so...

Biting back my scream, I forced myself to pivot and face the heat. My dragging feet moved me to the front of the ledge in front of the others.

"Backs against the wall, you two! Unless you want to die." I opened my water bottle and slopped it over my shoulder at Jessica's and Lobo's heads and chests. Any protests were lost in the forces of nature that boomed in my ears.

"If you've got any water left, use it. On yourself, lamebrain, not on me." I grabbed Jessica's bottle away that she aimed at my face and finished dousing her hair. Lobo's white teeth flashed in understanding...and also doubt. *Not enough aqua for that, terrorista.* But he wet his hair and emptied the rest over Jessica.

Now what? The heat burned intense. Even my teeth ached.

"Against the wall." I stayed in front of them and backed up. My feet slipped as Lobo rebelled and shoved back. His body didn't accept being sandwiched between a fanatic and the cliff. But he couldn't do much in the small space without knocking one of us off.

I kept backing, a shuffled centimeter at a time, until I felt their panting bodies squeezed together, pinned between my backpack and the rock. Lobo's hand pinched vise-like around my upper arm. There would be a bruise on the sword's hilt under the thick fur sleeve.

"You're smashing me. Let up!"

The insignificant hurt from Jessica's kick started the Gilead in my head. He began to rail at me. *Get away from these enemies! This is pointless suicide, Dove. Climb. Fly up this ridge. Escape. What are you doing, you idiot?*

He had a point. What was I doing?

Mother birds did this for their babies sometimes in wildfires. Covered them with their wings, so the nestlings underneath would live. My grandma had told me about finding a nest once and a mother's stretched remains that stunk like char.

I twisted out of Lobo's grip and spread my arms wide to become the mother bird.

Sometimes it stunk being the only one ready to die.

17

My attempt wasn't going to work. Maybe if I was huge like Stone, with a massive boulder of a body, I'd have a chance to save the others. Then I could have bought these two unsaved a couple more years before death and eternal damnation set in. But I was too puny to play a shield. My Armor was spiritual and couldn't protect against a physical assault. And the fire was too wild, too powerful. Too evil.

The buffeting wind eased the blistering heat against my face. It also made the fire contort and twist, more terrible than the heat. A surge of flames shot up, forming a monstrous forked object, a hand with flickering claws. The talons reached...and clenched shut, brushing the toes of my shoes.

Lobo shouted. My neck opening pulled tight as if Jessica grab my clothes, pulling me back into an impossible retreat, using me as a barrier.

The fiery claws swiped again. The distinctive odor of singed hair mixed with the other smoke.

My sword and shield arms remained rigid and in place. My muscles ached. I wouldn't let them fall.

Keep me strong, God. Be my strength. You promised...until the end! Have mercy on these two I can't save. Have mercy on Gilead—

My feet faltered in the sudden burst of wind. If it

wasn't for the grip someone had on my shirt, I would have blown over. Another gust of south-moving air screamed through the canyon. It ripped past me and knocked against the reaching fire.

The orange surged forward, punched the wind, and burst into a shower of falling flames. Jessica screamed, and my shirt collar no longer choked me. She had released her grip. I tottered but regained my balance. My arms abandoned their defensive position in order to beat fiery ash from my front and swipe embers from my hair that kept flying into my open mouth.

More wind collided with the wall of fire, this time feeding the inferno so it grew. The searing brightness towered high above me, a whirl of fire blocking the sky with its blinding force. Now the scorching tornado leaned backward...falling from me... forced away from my cliff.

The fire seemed to recognize its bullied retreat and made another furious lunge forward. But the wind blocked it. Even the lung-searing smoke wasn't allowed any nearer to me now.

God was my strength. My shield.

I trembled—but no longer with fear. My fist sliced the air. I waved my Sword of the Spirit high. "See God's power? He's not going to let you win, Satan. Get used to losing."

The fire's front line was reduced to burning the blackened desert it had already devoured. Without fuel, the blaze shrank to half its height. Through the heavy smoke, the defeated line of orange flickered, already dead at the eastern horizon.

Another gust blew past from the south. I closed my eyes to the steady stream cooling my sweat. Before

I opened them, wind hurtled from a new direction, above. It screamed over the top of the ridge, warning me to duck.

I obeyed.

The invisible forces of nature clashed, drove back the smoke, and then hit the distant line of flames. The winds continued to erase the pulsating orange, pushing it on all sides until it was contained. The raging wildfire that had chased us all day became a tight, burning ball a quarter mile away.

My hands clenched my waist where my invisible Belt of Truth wrapped tight. I shouted the truth. "And now...you die!"

The pulsating brightness kept its stubborn, squat form a moment longer. Then it began to move...to swirl...to spiral. A smoky haze settled around me, and I squinted through raw eyeballs at the fire pillar. The column swirled and stretched thinner and higher, becoming a pole, a thread...

Then it disappeared.

The charred, smoking desert became dark as if there'd been a sudden eclipse. The shrieking wind mutated to a moan. Green, dancing blobs blossomed in my vision at the spot where the fire had morphed into nothingness. I didn't shift on my own inky ledge. Without sight, I might plummet off.

But I laughed without sound. Even though my body was ragged and desperate for better air, I would stay here all night. This spot was holy. God had defended me on this ledge.

The forgotten bodies at my back forced me forward. In the camera's small light, I made out Jessica's red-rimmed eyes and swollen nose surrounded by her wet hair. The whites of Lobo's eyes and teeth were frozen open in shock. Both hands stayed locked on the camera that pointed in the direction of the defeated fire.

18

The night erupted into an unholy mess of noise and lights.

Two helicopters with spotlights appeared. Onboard the hovering craft with the word *RESCUE* blazed across its side, the uniformed strangers shouted instructions and extracted the camera crew. The one who landed on my ledge to assist with the airlift thrust the waiting harness at me. "Come on! You're holding us up! Let's get outta here!"

Savannah's face peered out at me from the other helicopter's open side. Her accusing finger pointed at my bunless hair that flapped from the speed of the helicopter's propeller.

I backed away from the uniformed pagan with the harness whose neck and ears were flushing red with impatience. "I'll climb by myself. I'm fine. I want to be alone—leave me alone!"

I pulled myself up and over the overhanging crag.

With a shrug and a signal to the others onboard, he hooked himself to the dangling equipment and departed.

My body sagged in the relative stillness. I breathed in the peace of being alone as I finished my solo climb. At the top, I forced my quivering leg muscles to sprint across the cliff's flat mesa. Still, I was unable to lose the helicopter's spotlight that made me like a bug under a glass.

I picked my way down the far side, still trapped in the circle of light. Even without the illumination, a toddler could make this descent. Even Jessica would have been able to survive it. Where was the challenge? Large fissures and stacked rock with comfy ledges turned the rock face into a playground.

My movements slowed as I approached the fluorescent flooded ground. Uniformed strangers raced through the smoky haze like ants sensing the harvest season ending.

"Oof." My feet hit the uneven ground, followed by my backside. I scurried away from the chaos. Using hand gestures, Savannah spoke to a uniformed man, but her eyes zeroed in on me. I wedged myself into a niche in the bluff's shadows.

A hand gripped my elbow. Lobo dragged me further away out of the light and into the night's veiling solitude. "You. Talk. What was that? Those fire shapes...that wind. Huh?"

He shook me. When I refused to explain or speak, he pivoted me against a nearby boulder. Now we were invisible to the others with only the faintest glow reaching us from around the huge, oblong rock.

"Huh, fanatic? You were talking to it."

"Lobo? Is that you? Both teams are taking off now since we're OK. I've got your equipment and a new tent." Jessica's figure appeared around the boulder, lugging bags and bulky objects.

She seemed oblivious to Lobo's jutted chin and angry stance. "Set up camp here?"

I dodged under his stiff arm.

"No. We keep walking." I scowled that my voice shook in relief. But part of me cheered that she hadn't given up and left me to finish the trek alone with this violent cameraman who demanded impossible answers.

Still, only one pair of footsteps followed me. I swung around. He leaned against the boulder with his arms crossed.

I flung up my own at Lobo's stubbornness. "You want answers, Lobo? Fine! You stay with me—both of you, no matter what—to the end. Lightning, hail, bees, snakes...whatever attacks, you don't duck out. You stay with me, and you'll discover what you want to know. More than you want to know. But I'm not failing and going back to the detention center and letting my brother die because you two ignorants get scared and run."

When I marched on, two sets of feet crunched in the gravelly dirt behind me. A cold, plastic bottle forced its way into my gritty palm. I raised it to my lips, tossing its cap and sucking down the clean-tasting water.

"Fanatics have brothers?" Lobo's bad mood had vanished with the sound of the first departing helicopter. "So, yours isn't as indestructible as you? What's he dying of?"

"Stupidity." My feet cut a wide detour to avoid the rattling of a snake on our left. But now I faced a star that sputtered through the thick haze straight ahead. *Flashflashflash.*

I threw down my belongings in the dirt, unable to stomach any more of Satan's traps tonight. "We'll make camp here. Clear your sleeping area of snakes."

The cameraman kept walking as if deaf. What was he doing? Could he do that? After a moment's hesitation, I chased after with Jessica at my heels. "You said you weren't allowed to lead."

"I'm not."

"Liar."

After another quarter of a mile, he ducked into a deep shadow against the side of the cliff. A camera light showed it to be an empty, shallow den. The blackened remains of an old campfire littered its entrance.

I grunted and threw my pack next to the char in the better, more protected spot than I'd picked to camp. "Lucky find."

He shrugged. "I might know this turf some. Lived in Laredo, a town near here, as a kid. I escaped to the wilderness when I could. Sometimes camped out here in the summers."

I settled against the still-warm rock, letting the others check for snakes and not bothering to dig out my fire starter. I'd had enough heat tonight.

My index finger played with the worn edge of the paper in my sock. It was easy to picture a younger Lobo out here in the barren, arid landscape. Hungry. Thirsty. Surviving. He belonged out here, like I did in the trees.

He disappeared out of the den's mouth and returned holding vegetation—pole-like pieces as tall as a child, covered with sharp spines. He flung these at the opening and left again. Before Jessica had finished eating her bag of jerky meat, he'd created a fencelike barrier that extended our enclosure's mouth.

Dusting his palms, he settled at the fire remains. "I always sleep better behind Devil's Walking Stick. Good stuff. Keeps out curious predators, and their flowers have a tasty tang. Sorry to raise your hopes high, Dove. They're not in season now."

I reached for my pathetic food supply. "Bet you've

eaten more cacti than I have."

"A few. But they're not as tasty as the ratones...or smoked hoppers. I know you've still got a stash. Been hungering for them all day. Hand some over, and I'll give you a fruit bar. Just don't tell my boss." He winked at Jessica, who blinked as if she disapproved. "Here. Catch."

After the few seconds it took me to peel the foil wrapper off, my taste buds ached from the tart fruit and sweet deliciousness. Best trade of my life.

Jessica pushed my open bag away from herself with her boot. "Yuck. She has to eat bugs because it's that or starve. But you, Wolf...that's sick. You're crazy."

I choked. "Wolf?"

"My name, terrorista. Lobo. 'Wolf' in Spanish. You know, arrooo, arrooooooooooo?"

He broke off his realistic howling that made my insides squeeze together. "Now how about those promised answers? Jesse saw it, too, so don't say what happened out there was natural. Because what we saw was some freaky wind and fire doing battle with you commanding the troops."

I reclosed my pack and stuck it under my head. "Tomorrow. In the morning, I'll explain then...yeah."

Jessica pressed her black earplugs into her canals. "You'd better." Her head began to bop, though her pupils didn't shift from me.

I turned my back to the speck of light outside the entrance, flashing in the distance. And to Wolf and Jesse. The two new nonbelievers—with the same Heathen names—that God had shoved into my life.

Lobo's joints cracked as if he stretched. "Yes. Morning...I can wait until morning. And after you reveal the mysteries of the fire battle, we can discuss this crazy business of the night sky. When I camp alone for many years, I see stars and a moon. When we camp together, new stars appear, old ones fall, and a certain one dances. Yes, dances, terrorista. Like it is doing now."

19

Lobo eyed me from his bright pool of sunshine. He leaned against the edge of the den's entrance next to the pile of needled vegetation. Steam from the mug he gripped joined the lingering haze from yesterday and wafted around him.

I sniffed. Smoke and...*what*? My nose detected a strong animal stench. I inhaled again. A strong stench. Animal mixed with something rusty...metallic. Blood?

I jolted upright, no longer sleepy, and grabbed up my belongings I'd used as a head cushion. I touched the maroon patch drying black on my bag's woven material. My hands flew to my hair, then my face. Fine. They were both fine, neither responsible for the red stain.

So if the blood wasn't mine...

My eyes roamed over the others. Were they hurt? My heart thumped against my ribs at the thought. Jessica lay asleep, breathing slow. No bright puddles or splashes were in her vicinity to indicate an animal had attacked.

Lobo's eyebrows raised.

Was he injured? He seemed healthy, except for a cut that disappeared into his short scruff of a beard and his scratched-up knuckles. And how would his blood get on my backpack if he'd been bleeding in the night? Unless he had left it when he searched for answers I hadn't yet given him, answers he thought I might have hidden under my grasshopper stash.

He sipped from his plastic mug without breaking eye contact. My nails scratched my foot...my ankle...then they bumped the paper's edge. Its folded angle seemed to be in the position I'd left it last night.

I lobbed my pack at him, but this time it wasn't to trade food items. "What's this junk smeared on my stuff? And my clothes?" I now saw my clothes were splattered with it, too. The dark fur stuck up—stiff, matted, and darker in spots.

Lobo leaned over and rubbed at the stain with his finger. "So, that's the stink. It's blood mixed with...it's a familiar...something."

I glared at his ignorance and then past his ear at the closest rock formation, less than an hour's walk away and bright with the sun. Its top ran flat, exposed, and bare. There was no hint of the Amhebran coder who had signaled me for hours last night.

I bit my lip. "I don't like it. Why—"

"Why indeed?" Lobo held his camera, directing it at the bluff I scrutinized. He gestured with the cattail boom for me to continue speaking. I shook my head.

"Answers, terrorista. You promised me."

I flicked my chin at the camera. *Not while that electronic is on.* I would tell him and Jessica what they wanted to know because I'd said I would and because I needed them for my brother's sake. But I owed the rest of the world nothing. Less than nothing.

I cut short our argument by shouldering my ruined pack, stepping over the knee-high pile of Devil's Walking Stick, and heading into the pale sunshine. Leaving Lobo to shake Jessica awake and scramble after me when he could.

~*~

Two days left. An irrational pang of something similar to panic accompanied this knowledge. I had two days to reach my destination of civilization.

Crinkle. I'd wrapped Ruth's paper in the plastic from the food bar for a sweat barrier. It betrayed me again with that small sound. But the others didn't glance at my ankle.

How could they not hear the distinct, suspicious, food-wrapper crackle when my ankle bent? The desert around us stretched too silent. As if every bird and insect had left us behind, chased away by the recent smoke. Each of our noises seemed big and clumsy in the scorching air that clung heavy and expectant with our needs.

We all needed something. Lobo, explanations to the miracles. Jessica, more footage since her camera stuck on me like tree sap. And me, to be out of here.

Two days left.

Stress sweat trickled down the tracks made by my normal sweat. The combination blinded me so I almost missed the tiny carcasses in the wide chasm I followed south.

"Ratones?" Lobo knelt and touched one.

There were six rodents, arranged in a neat, manmade pile. Their bodies' stiffness revealed they'd been killed an hour ago—or less since they were untouched by any predator, including the mountain lion I'd seen evidence of. I straightened and almost trod on a mushroom-sized, circular object, also in the dust. Its scratched, plastic face glinted like dull glass.

Jessica rescued it. "A compass. Broken but..."

She handed it to me. I stared down at the unmoving clock-like hand pointing at the SE. Southeast. It stayed at SE, no matter which direction I swiveled while holding it in front of myself.

Both the crew were looking way too expectantly at me in the stillness, as if I had an explanation for the dead rats and broken litter.

I shunted the useless compass back to Jessica and trudged on through the thick heat. My feet traced a dried-up stream's path. Didn't people build towns next to water sources?

It was a weak plan.

Show me. Show me my way, God.

The others scoured the dusty path we hiked with wasteful energy. Examining the prickly brush as if we were on a treasure hunt. Did pagan kids play that game? Each fall, my mom and aunt used to hide shiny pennies for me, my brother, and cousins to find. The scattered trails of copper always led to the same place—the vegetable beds—where we kids would holler in pretend surprise and dig for the caches of pennies that'd been buried with the spring seeds. We threw the potatoes and carrots into harvested piles as we worked, flinging dirt at each other, too. I still had my jar of pennies on my shelf next to my hammock, waiting to be spent. They were no longer shiny but green.

But now, the only prize I hunted was a sign of Heathen life. A road. A car. A building. Not anything I would find under a spiky yucca plant. I wouldn't stop to rest tonight. I couldn't camp until I found that manmade sight that marked civilization. My ticket for home tomorrow.

The leather water pouch, the one I'd held twice before, leaned against a prickly pear to my right. I strode past with my nose in the air.

"Not a small smile, terrorista Dove? Not even for this?" Lifting it, Lobo sniffed, took a swig, and tried to hand the container to me. "OK. Then I pour it away."

I snatched the pouch from him, using two hands because it was heavy. Under his scrutiny, I guzzled half of its weight then grunted.

Good water this time. A casual glance revealed no footprints in the dust between rocks. Neither human's nor cat's. Where had the lion gone? I'd observed its tracks all morning. Had it left, or had we hiked out of its territory? Or had it circled behind to stalk us in stealth?

I stunk like roadkill, thanks to the bloody offering I'd been tagged with. What carnivore out here wouldn't keep tabs on a free meal? No, it probably stalked us.

I peeped again at the ground. Nope, no shoeprint.

The one, unfamiliar print I'd sighted today had been too small for Stone's foot. The discovery had eased the knot in my stomach...but it also made me hang my head for having suspected him of being the bad water giver.

Someone else was out here besides us and Stone. Who? Why did the person leave me rats, trash, and water?

Where are you, Stone? Did you escape the fire?

Yes. Of course he had. I wouldn't—couldn't—mourn another person that I didn't hate.

~*~

The sun veered for the western horizon as if exhausted and ready to be done shining for the day.

"You take a break and wait here. I'll be right back." I tossed my bag into the shade made by brambly sticks.

Lobo settled and sucked down water, but Jessica trailed after me toward a sky-reaching, crumbly rock formation a few yards away.

After you? I mock gestured at the column. Then I started up alone, frowning when the food wrapper in my sock rustled against the rock's rough surface.

It was a dizzying climb, but with water circulating my body again I reached the top without a lethal fumble. But even up so high, I wasn't alone. I ignored the cameras directed at me and scrutinized the horizons. Formations, like the one I balanced on, flowed in a depressing monotone to each horizon with no relief.

No town.

No road.

No wildcat.

No Stone.

Something flashed. Further south and near the horizon closest to the setting sun, a sharp glint struck my eye. A reflective object, possibly metal or glass.

Breathing fast, I scrambled higher...higher than was safe, even for a tree dweller. I craned off my iffy stone perch, one hand a visor at my brow.

A building crouched low in the dust. Its metallic roof glinted at me above a smear of white paint. A few inches away, half-hidden behind a jumble of rocks, sat another square-sided, man-made structure. A building in a town.

Civilization.

20

Lobo handed me a pinecone-sized, grilled chunk of meat still recognizable as a rat from the pile. "If I was the fanatic, I'd check out the town tonight. At least walk the perimeter. With no sun, the journey will be as easy as—"

A distant, feline scream ended his pointless suggestion.

I picked my dinner off its tiny skeleton. "Nope. The Savannah lady said day fourteen. Meet her on day fourteen. That's tomorrow. I don't want to break some weird rule I don't know about by getting to the spot early."

Outside this stacked-rock enclosure, beyond the next ridge lay my journey's finish line. Was it relief that made me so chatty now?

The camera people exchanged head shakes. Then Lobo shrugged. He settled next to me at the fire. He nudged my shoe with his. "Answers. You promised."

Jessica claimed the small space between us. For once, she didn't hold her camera. Instead, it rested a few feet away on a short, three-stick base. A light shone out from the part of it directed at me. The electronic was on. The cattail boom rested across her knees.

Before I had refused to explain with the unsaved world listening. But why had I cared? Believe me...don't believe me...as long as Lobo and Jessica did or at least considered what I had to say.

I stretched, bumping against Jessica's shoulder. The fact that the nonbelievers didn't recoil from my accidental touches, and I didn't scoot away from theirs, maybe that meant something. Governor Ruth could be right. Maybe I was 'Heathen inclined.' Comfortable among my enemies.

Too comfortable.

I braced for the chain reaction inside of me that this knowledge might set off. Like this winter when I'd lain sleepless and stared at the stars while banishing Jezebel and Wolfe from my thoughts. I'd gripped the edges of my hammock and prayed I'd never have to risk losing myself to the world again.

I yawned and sipped from the leather pouch. "Answers?"

"The fire and wind battle. Start with those."

"Well, obviously you know the first part, why the fire was after us like that."

Both expressions remained blank. After another mouthful, I explained, enunciating like I did for Jovie when she chose to act like a brainless infant. "Because...? Satan? Uh...he attacked?"

A snort echoed. "Excuse me, terrorista. You're saying Satan started the wildfire. The devil. As in, 'Aha, those look like some good people to burn up today.' And the devil rubbed two sticks. And lit the fire?"

I rubbed my grimy forehead with my free hand. "You make it sound improbable when you say it like that. No, it's more like Satan got someone else, a real human being, to set the fire for him and then used it to—"

"Who?"

I frowned. I'd been obsessing on the "who" for days. "It doesn't matter who. What matters is that Satan was behind the person's actions. He's the puppet master controlling the human puppet. And then, of course, God sent the wind to drive the fire away because it wasn't His plan for us to die right then. And in the end, He crushed the devil's attacking force. God saved the three of us."

Lobo shook his black hair and chortled into the fire, not a nice laugh. "If you'd heard as many religious fanatics as I have—everyone with their stories about their 'powerful gods' and their rules for the good boys and girls of earth to get blessed. And how to get to Utopia...or heaven...or whatever you want to call it. If you'd heard it like I have, then you'd understand. Yours is the same story with a different set of rules about how to hang out with the same boring God and tap into His questionable power to—"

I hurled my bones into the embers. They bounced out. "You're wrong. Christianity isn't about the rules."

Jessica pulled a sharp breath between her teeth and pushed the black, furry cattail at me. "There are no rules?"

"I'll tell you if he's done insulting my God." I took a deep breath.

Words. Give me Your words.

My anger faded. They had to understand. "Christianity isn't about what you or I do. That's why it's not the same story as everyone else's. It's about what God has done for us—loving us so much that He sent His own Son, Jesus, to earth to live and die and be our Savior. All we have to do is accept His free gift— that His son defeated death for us. That's it. There's nothing else we have to do but choose Him and His side."

Lobo smirked, his handsome face twisted ugly in the fire's glow. "Ahhh...love. You speak of love. You have a God that loves you so much He had you detained at a CTDC. And then sent you to a desert where you know squat about surviving. Yes. That's real loving."

"Did I die?" I waited for his response that didn't come. Then I smirked back. "And He provided for me every single time I might have been hurt or killed. God can handle Texas, even if I can't. So don't forget to show that part of the episode to those nonbelievers watching. I don't care what you tell them about me. But you'd better tell them right about my God. Don't you dare lie."

He waved a lazy hand. "I'm impartial. You're telling all that now. But you're sidestepping the main issue that I—the viewers—need to understand. Now you explain this. How did you unleash your God's power? Tell how you controlled the wind and—"

"I didn't. I have no power over the wind or weather. Or the stars. I did nothing." I yawned huge, pulled my blankets from my belongings, and flopped down.

"Nothing. She did nothing. You hear that Jesse?"

Jessica rose. Distinctive noises of her putting her equipment away for the night bounced from the walls of our rock enclosure. Outside, the mountain lion called again. I pulled my metallic blankets around my body tighter with a loud rustling.

"You're afraid." He laughed.

I poked my head out. "Nope."

"You shouldn't be. In fact, you should feel a sister

connection to cougars. They're like you. They get a bad rap. They go out of their way to leave us humans alone. And they only attack when provoked. Like you. Harmless. You agree?"

He poked the fire with his long branch of Devil's Walking Stick while another scream bounced off the vast mesa formations in the night. He sighed and threw his stick onto the others already piled high at the shelter's entrance. "I'll take first watch."

21

My head spun. My left hand gripped the wooden sign, *Welcome to Shafter, Texas*. The rickety structure groaned in protest against my full weight.

Another town's welcome sign flashed across my blurring vision, the one in Wolfe and Jezebel Pickett's hometown of Sisters. That one was flanked with flowers like a garden box from Eden. This one looked like a grave marker where cacti gathered to mourn and die.

Shielding my eyes against the pounding sun I gazed at my civilization—the town of Shafter, Texas—at the piles of rock debris that had once been walls and the dry grass and bushes that filled the expanses where roads should have been.

A lopsided board propped on a weedy cement block summed the place up with its two painted words: *Ghost Town*.

I didn't have to worry about the town's residents attacking me for parading down its Main Street. Shafter had no Main Street. And no residents left in this shell of a town.

The cameras stayed on my face. The camera people's panting from our hurried climb out of the chasm was as loud as their unspoken words. I heard them, smug after my declaration last night of how loving my God was. How He never failed me.

He's failed you.

I pushed off the sign and meandered in the direction of the only real building in this town, the white one with the reflective roof. From a distance, the building had fooled me into believing this was civilization. For a moment, I'd thought this was the spot where I was supposed to complete my journey, fulfill my end of the legal contract, and meet my ride back to Oregon to save my brother and stop the Reclaim's violence.

My feet scuffed to a stop. A gurgle of laughter swelled in my throat. Here before me, rising from the sun-bleached weeds, was the boarded-up entrance of the large, peeling-paint structure with its cross-shaped belfry on top. This treacherous building that had lured me here with its rusting, metal roof was…a church.

I chuckled.

"Um. Terrorista?"

"She's slaphappy, Lobo. Look at her."

I continued to drink in the weathered, broken-down structure. A relic of the long ago Christian gatherings throughout the nation my grandparents had known, even though I never had.

A looseness flowed through my limbs and spread through the rest of my body. The comforting sensation covered me, as if someone had wrapped me in my favorite blanket and soothed me in Gran's old willow rocker.

Gran. Oh, Gran.

My fist clenched over my heart, my smile faded, and the last of my hysteria fizzled away.

A whisper drew my eyes to the glassless, arched window. *This way.*

Grandma's beacon. She had followed the Holy

Spirit confidently, faithfully, even accepting death with courage. And the Spirit wanted me to follow with the same amount of faith. I jumped, grabbed the windowsill, and threw my first leg over.

Both feet sank through the rotten floorboards of the deserted church. Beams of light poured through holes in the ceiling, revealing the place to be a disaster zone. Broken glass. Overturned, warped benches. Piles of rocks sprouting weeds. A large, metal piece of roofing curling up from the rubble on the ground.

Yet the love that believers had once put into this church still echoed. The evidences of their devotion were hidden...but present still beneath all the grime.

When had the Christians abandoned this church? At the Purge? Perhaps even after. Because wouldn't seventy years of neglect look worse than this?

My mind straightened the wrecked benches into tidy rows and cleared away the debris. It pieced the curled metal back into the opening in the ceiling. The honey-colored, oak floor planks all ran the same direction, supporting the figures who kneeled upon them. The brave remnant of my people. They were the Christians who endured and met here after our country decided to persecute them as terrorists. They sang hymns and risked their lives for this gathering place. Until they lost their earthly battle.

I'd only encountered one other church before. That one in Oregon had been beautiful. Big enough to hold hundreds. And evil...a plaything of Satan's. Time and nature had faded this church's beauty, but the goodness, God's presence, still remained.

I sank onto an upright bench near the glassless window and bowed my head. Lobo made a lot of noise as he dropped over the sill and helped Jessica over.

Broken glass and gravel ground against floorboards, and a smell of dry rot filled my nose. The bench groaned when the camera crew settled next to me, one on either side.

I shook my head and examined my dirty cuticles. I didn't want to talk or for them to talk.

"Listen. You need to keep walking. Find the—"

"Lobo," Jessica warned.

"—the road. Yes, there's a road. This is off the record—I'm not telling you this. But you'll find the road if you keep walking. Not many cars come this way, but if you're lucky, one will. It'll take you to Big Bend National Park. You're only eighty miles from where you need to be, real civilization. You can't walk it in time, but that's only two hours of driving."

"Lobo, quit telling her this stuff. And no one is going to pick her up. Look at her."

Lobo stayed silent. I hadn't seen my reflection in days, but I could imagine what I looked like: a filthy, starved, desperate Christian in ragged fur. And I figured I didn't smell too great either.

Should I trust Lobo and search for a road? I sat in a soft haven out of the hard, afternoon heat. And even if I could make myself move from this spot and force my blistered feet to take me to pavement, Jessica wasn't lying. No one would ever let me into their vehicle.

I cracked open my eyes. Lobo's stubbled chin jutted, and he leaned around me. "She needs to get to the road."

"Yeah? Well I may be new to all this filming of the fanatic, but I remember there are rules we agreed to. We're not supposed to help her figure out—"

"Why was my journey so much harder than the others'?" My quiet question halted their argument. "I only saw a couple of other religious people on television, but their struggles were for water, food, and shelter. Why was mine so much worse? Was it because you all hate me so much? Because I'm a Christian? I answered your questions last night. Now you answer mine. You don't even have to explain how your people did it all—with the bugs, the flood, the fire, the poisoned water—"

I broke off at my mention of water. They didn't know about my nighttime visits to the water giver. Or did they? Was that part of the whole setup as well, part of the viewers' entertainment?

"Dehydration. No water. That was your only obstacle from us. That and—"

"Lobo!"

"—and you not making it to civilization. There are three visitor centers in Big Bend Park." He continued to speak despite Jessica's attempt to silence him. "From the beginning, I gave you a thousand-to-one chance of finding a campground or ranger station, let alone that you'd do it in time. The most direct trek was over seventy miles. After we were holed up for four days by the hoppers, you had zero chance."

I nodded. "But you weren't going to stop me from trying. Watching me try was...fun."

"The whole time you were heading too far west. Yesterday, when you found that broken compass, I thought you'd take the hint. You'd head southeast. No, I didn't plant it, Jesse. It was only a coincidence, so relax. But it was too late by then anyway. Unless you'd gotten to a road. And it's not too late for that, Dove. Right now."

Heaviness settled in a bar across my shoulders. Invisible hands kept me where I curled up on the warped wooden bench.

"Don't expect me to feel bad for you. You're the one who agreed to take on this challenge. So why did you?" Jessica's camera was on me again, her voice aggressive and strangely angry.

"Was it to get out of the detention center?" Lobo's question was thoughtful.

I started to nod but paused mid-bob.

"I wonder if you agreeing had something to do with helping your brother who's dying of stupidity?"

My lips twitched at Lobo's assumption. It wasn't too far off the mark. Then they formed one word. "Rebecca."

"Rebecca? Who's she? Your sister?"

I shut my mouth. I'd said too much.

They persisted in badgering me with questions. Dumb ones that didn't matter. Lobo began to coax me—and then threaten me—to find the road. It was yards away, he said. So easy to find. So much smarter than sitting here. But after a couple hours of this, he put his heavy water bottle and a fruit bar in my lap and stood.

While the helicopter passed again overhead, the crew wandered around the confines of the church relic. I dozed off as they shifted broken stuff, exploring and exclaiming over what surfaced in the remains.

Jessica gave a strangled shriek. I jerked upright.

She perched, frozen on a pile of rubble, lit by the late afternoon sun streaming down from the hole in the roof. Next to her, Lobo clutched a foot-long, wooden cross he must've uncovered. Both stared at the glassless window. Balanced under its arch, a mountain lion poised on the weathered sill.

Stand together.

I slid off my bench that held the camera equipment. The cougar's tawny body stayed put. Only its reflective eyes pursued me as I took my spot in front of the other two in the stab of light.

"Yah! Yah! Run away!"

Lobo's wild shout failed. The cougar didn't flinch or turn.

"These cats, they stay away from us humans. From loud noises. From other cats. One cat catches another's marking scent and *pfft*. It turns tail and runs." Lobo's conversational murmur drifted from behind me. "Terrorista? Now I know what scent you're wearing. Cougar catnip."

A rock clattered down the pile behind me, loud and echoing, as if displaced by a foot.

"If she's baited with catnip, then why are we standing behind her?"

"Shh, Jesse. Softly. But yes, that is something I, too, am wondering."

Bam. Bam. Bang. Someone began to hammer on the boarded-up door. Poised at the opposite wall, the cat's ears went back. It leaped forward onto an overturned bench and sauntered closer. The yellow, dilated eyes zoned in on mine.

"Lobo!" It was Savannah's voice from the other side of the door. "Lobo, why can't I get you on your radio? You don't turn it off. That's not OK. Tell me, Lobo! Is the fanatic still with you? And Jessica? We promised her father..."

A creaking bang. She, or someone with her, was prying the boards off the front entrance barricade.

"Dove Pickett!"

Bang. Scraaape. Savannah's voice came out more breathless now. "Dove Pickett. You have failed to reach civilization in our agreed upon fourteen-day time period. You have created a breach of contract..."

Outside the accusation droned on. From inside, now at the foot of the rubble pile, the cougar crouched low.

And from the rusty-edged hole overhead, a black-haired guy hurtled down through sunlit dust mites and landed square on the creature's tawny back.

22

Wolfe's extremities flailed, then tightened around the enraged cougar's back.

"Whoa, whoa...whoa!" He strained to keep his flushed face out of range of the snarling, yellow teeth and unsheathed claws.

Lobo streaked forward. The cross in his fist became a club. As it connected with the furry skull, the feline screamed, and Wolfe let go. He squirmed away.

The cameraman delivered another blow with his cross, and the sleek body pulled out of the fray. It gave me one backward glance. In three bounds the cat reached the arched window and disappeared. Someone outside shouted.

Jessica shoved me. Her wiry arms and sharp elbows kept me away from Wolfe, who struggled to sit up. Blood trailed down one brown arm.

"Wolfe—"

At my cry, Lobo about-faced and charged back up the pile of broken cement. He grabbed me around the waist. "Three, two, one!" With incredible strength, he lifted and launched me skyward.

Midair, I screamed.

Strong hands caught me inches below the ceiling. They locked around my wrists and pulled me straight up. My head cleared the ragged, metal hole in the roof. My body followed, unscratched.

I stared at Stone, who stayed crouched and half-holding me. His body underneath his leather tunic was rigid and unmoving, as if he was as surprised as I was to find myself in his arms. Stone was here in Texas with Wolfe?

Boards clattered to the ground below, superseded by an explosion of shouting. No doubt the helicopter crew, Savannah included, had made it inside the church. Jessica called out. I didn't hear Lobo.

Stone slid me from his lap onto the hot tin roof. With a sigh, he bent over the hole. A second later Jezebel's brother swung into sight, dripping blood. He released Stone's hand and shook out his own.

"Ready to fly, Dove Bird? Follow me." Wolfe leaped to the roof's edge, sat down, and slid off feet first. *Thud.* He'd hit the ground.

A feline's cry stopped the voices inside the church. I held my breath. Beneath the metal burning my palms, someone whispered a question about predators.

Stone signaled that I relocate to Wolfe's exit spot. I inched to the roof's edge until I could peer over.

My jaw dropped. Half-hidden behind a Devil's Walking Stick bush, Melody waved up at me. Next to her, a taller and darker-skinned person wearing a headscarf and sunglasses sat astride a bicycle. Rebecca gave me a cool thumbs-up. Wolfe gestured at me with his blood-streaked arm to hurry up.

No cougar lurked anywhere in sight.

Sky alive, had it been Melody screaming like a cat just now? She was gifted—I'd forgotten how gifted. Wolfe windmilled both his injured and non-injured arms. *Jump!* His face squinched with laugher.

A bolder voice from inside the building barked a question. Running footsteps crunched toward the church's entrance.

Whoosh. My breath left me. Stone had picked me up and now launched us off the church's roof together. On the pebbly ground, he set me on my feet. Then, as if having second thoughts, he scooped me up and jogged, heading for the others beside the vegetation.

"I can walk, I can—Wait. What's that for?" I pointed at the green bicycle with fat tires leaning on the other side of the tall plant. My heart raced, and I struggled to get down.

"Hold on, Stone. She's supposed to ride with me. We agreed." Wolfe, sitting on his gray bicycle, didn't smile now.

"Don't fight." Rebecca pulled at her scarf so her lips showed. "Wolfe, she'll ride with him since you're hurt. Get on Stone's bike, Dove. Balance on the bar in front or sit behind him on the seat. Decide how you want to ride. Now."

I eased onto the object I hated more than most things on earth. Stone held it steady. "Easy there. Easy."

"Dove Pickett!" Savannah's voice carried out the empty window and across the rocks and dust. I whipped my feet up onto the bicycle's frame.

"Danger," Melody whimpered.

"Shut up saying that. We know."

I whirled around, raising my eyebrows at Rebecca.

Her long fingers clenched the bicycle's front bar where Melody now balanced. They moved in a strangling motion around the rubber handles. "I mean, please stop warning us, Brae. It's unhelpful. We're already aware."

"Danger," the girl in front of her mouthed.

Wolfe threw Stone another dagger look. "Fine."

He propelled his own gray frame on wheels forward. Sandy soil sprayed from his back tire at us.

Stone waited for the girls to follow, and then we too weaved around yuccas, dead plants, and rocks. The ghost town slid by in a bumpy blur. Crumbling rock walls. The shell of a boarded-up gas station. A decrypted post office.

The barren desert hills loomed bigger. For so many days they'd represented evil and my entrapment. Now they were freedom. Safety and escape.

Crack.

A gunshot deafened me. A grizzled man clutching a shotgun appeared from the dust. His tan overalls camouflaged him against the rise in the ground and the lean-to shelter made of rough boards.

In front of me, Stone's wide body lurched with the gun's report. The tires below us skidded, and the ground rose up. A bush of dead sticks cushioned my rolling, face-first fall. Before I'd tumbled to a full stop, Stone lifted me, his hands encircling my forearms.

"You OK, Dove? Argh." He released me back into the bush and grabbed his elbow, where dark red began to seep.

"Oh, no, Stone! Stone's been shot. He's been shot!" Melody cried through splayed fingers. My other two rescuers were ahead of us, frozen but still upright. And beyond them, behind the sneering gunman, a familiar figure with dark hair sprinted around a clump of bushes. Lobo stopped short, his chest heaving.

As I checked to make sure I hadn't lost my message in my fall, a satisfied cackle halted me. With uneven footsteps, the old man limped nearer to us, his gun in his grip. He paused on a pile of lava rocks. For what seemed like an eternity he stood there, pointing his barrel at each of us in turn. *Eenie. Meenie. Miny. Moe.*

Unaware that Lobo was sneaking up behind him, he nodded at me and raised the shotgun's butt to his armpit.

23

Lobo hurled himself onto the gunman.

"Ugh!" Both men hit the ground with an ugly sound of flesh and bone against rock. They thrashed and wrestled against a boulder until the bearded stranger flopped over and lay still. Lobo scrambled up, grabbed the fallen shotgun, and whirled to face us. Stone, who'd been frozen, lurched in front of me, still clasping his elbow.

"Go on!" Lobo swung back around and pointed the weapon at the sprawled, unconscious figure. "Go! Before he wakes up. Before the others...go on!"

The gray bicycle wheeled around Stone and pulled up next to me. Wolfe made a sympathetic clucking noise. "Shot, huh? Hope you'll make it OK." His chipper tone implied the opposite.

Before Stone could reply, his long nose wrinkled. "Whew. C'mon, Dove. Try this perch."

The giant's narrowed eyes stayed on Wolfe's arm as it came around and steadied me on the front bar of his bicycle. Then we shot forward, and Stone vanished out of sight behind us.

"They have a helicopter." I pointed at the wide, blue sky, still free of flying machines. But for how long? "It's brainless to try to outride them."

We moved slower up a bumpy incline between prickly clumps.

"That'd be true. If they had...a working...copter. Or a...radio. Used my...E...M...P." He grunted the letters of the power-killing technology he'd let off. I glanced over my shoulder at him.

He stood on the pedals while pumping his legs up and down. His mouth hung open, and he gasped. "Quit...throwing off...our balance. Sit still."

I bit my lip and held on tighter. The bar under my backside tossed me up and caught me with each bump. My sweaty palms slipped. I couldn't hang on much longer. "Faster, Wolfe."

Yards away Melody perched in front of Rebecca on a maroon bicycle. Her Brae eyes stayed shut but her mouth moved, as if whimpering. Rebecca's scarf sagged, revealing her gritted teeth and lots of sweat. Like Wolfe, she stood while pedaling. It looked tiring.

Was Stone able to keep up?

I faced the hills ahead without finding out. But yes, of course the Bender brother was OK, even if he had a little blood on his elbow. And Lobo was fine, too. By this time, he would have sneaked back to Savannah and the crew. Would they find out he'd helped me so much? What would happen to him?

"Stay still...or...we'll eat dirt."

My gaze darted sideways in an attempt to see out the back of my skull.

Why had Lobo helped me? And how had he known Stone was on the roof? The way he threw me up like that...he'd known.

Through all my confusion, one clear fact rose to the front of my brain: Wolfe had blown out their electrical power with his EMP. Which meant no helicopter. And no car...for anybody.

I groaned in understanding. No car. We were

bicycling back to Oregon.

~*~

We stopped short of Oregon—still deep in the Texan wilderness...but far enough out of the EMP's range that Wolfe's jeep still worked. Low music with a beat issued from the vehicle's white frame, visible beneath its camouflage of sticks and scattered handfuls of sand. Splashing echoed from the pool at the bottom of a shallow crevice nearby.

I rung out my wet hair, my hands awkward without longer strands to coil. Not just my hands were restless. My whole body fidgeted in the featherweight, factory-made clothes I'd put on after washing. They were so soft. So cool. So inappropriate. I rubbed my exposed sword and shield tattoos, trying to cover them with my scrawny fingers.

Rebecca eyed me from the Jeep's seat where she reclined in the shade. "Cool. Time to head home."

She bopped her head. Under her bushy hair, she wore a calm that was at odds with the maniacal drumming of the music. But her kid brother, Joshua, was music-gifted. He probably slept with drumsticks the way Trinity used to sleep with a stuffed squirrel. Maybe the drumming reminded her of home.

Melody paused from dabbing water onto Stone's pale forehead. She pointed at the gray bandage on his thick arm, already showing red again. "Don't you think it's bad for him to move when he's so weak?"

Rebecca's calm flickered. As Wolfe heaved himself out of the crevice and shook like a dog, she began to explain, again, that it would be best for him to be closer to real medical care...in case.

Drops from Wolfe's hair and from his immodest, almost nonexistent shirt splattered me, while water from his cut-off pants pooled around his bare toes. He leaned in. His thin nose sniffed in my ear.

I kicked at him. "Go smell yourself."

His sunburnt shoulders shook, just like they had when Rebecca had suggested we spend a few extra minutes here to get his and Stone's wounds bandaged. The real reason we'd lingered by this water hole was because I'd needed to wash. Because I'd stunk.

"So, Dove. You make friends this week?"

I shrugged.

"Anyone...familiar to you?" He waited for my reply, which didn't come. He grinned. "We'll talk about this later. When you're in a less crummy mood. Here. Eat something."

He picked up a bright food bag from the ground, shoved it at me, and sauntered in the direction of his Jeep. But in a blink, Stone stood before him. The massive body blocked him from the vehicle's door on the driver's side where Rebecca reclined.

Wolfe's wet frame pulled up short. "You can't drive. Remember? You're wounded. Wounded and weak."

Stone pointed to the scratch on Wolfe's forearm that still oozed red. "So are you. And even with no arms, mine would still be stronger."

Lines pulled together on Wolfe's forehead in his obvious attempt to figure that one out. Then he swiped the blood at his wrist and stood taller. "It's my Jeep, so I'm driving."

The giant ignored this and offered a steady hand to Rebecca. He would help her down and take her place.

Melody skittered over to his side. "Why does it matter who owns what? Stone should drive."

Rebecca refused the hovering hand. "I disagree. And what do you even own, Melody?"

I chewed my broken thumbnail. I'd been trapped in a car with Stone before. I'd been thrown off my seat. Then there'd been the screaming and breaking glass and...

I backhanded the branch blocking the side of the Jeep. It fell to the ground. "Wolfe's driving. Get in." I scrambled over the open side into the back. I settled my pack, wet from its scrubbing, between my knees.

Wolfe unburied us from the desert camouflage, flinging sticks wide in his victory. He'd been chosen to drive. Rebecca slid over to let him into the seat. Stone and Melody, after a whispered side conversation, piled into the back where I waited. I ended up wedged in the area at their feet.

Melody sniffed. "That was unfair, Dove."

I shrugged. Stone was a big boy. He'd get over not driving.

He eyed me from under his bleached brows until Rebecca threw a brown tarp over my head and body. This was for my protection, she said. The tarp would keep me hidden from both hunters and passersby.

Already my rescue gave me a headache. Not only from the brutal bicycle ride and now the suffocating tarp, but because almost every non-family member I knew had come to get me out of Texas, which was mind blowing and stressful. Only an imbecile would have missed the tense lines dividing my group of rescuers and severing whatever harmony the group had started with.

Stone and Wolfe's reciprocated dislike? I wasn't drop-jawed over that. But Rebecca's rudeness to Melody? And let's face it, if I recognized rudeness, then someone was being rude.

But I wouldn't cry for the Brae girl. She was clingy, dependent, and...

What was Melody? She was my friend who had formed a relationship with someone else in the group.

Melody and Stone. An alliance existed between those two.

I fidgeted in my hiding place. Finally, I poked my head out from the stuffy air and eyed them. They sat less than a foot apart in the twilight, but at least they weren't holding hands. Not yet.

No. I wouldn't be like Reed. I shook my head to clear it and spoke to the vehicle in general. "So? I'm assuming you're not all here to tour southwestern ghost towns?"

The tension shifted. Rebecca began to talk. For a few minutes no one argued, and I got explanations—or at least enough facts—that I began to understand my last two confusing weeks.

I'd been right about Rebecca. She had known back in Oregon that I would fly to Texas to be a participant in *Fanatic Surviving*. My friend, the traitor, had set up the whole deal. The filming studio was located in Portland. She "knew people," and me doing this deal was the best way to get me out of the Christian Terrorist Detention Center.

I snorted in disbelief. She flipped her sunglasses down.

"Well, Rebecca, at least you had brains enough not to trust that 'your people' would let me go after two weeks like they'd promised. So, you worked your magic. Somehow you all swarmed together, and then you fished me out of that old church. Dumb question...but how did you know I'd be at that ghost town?"

Wolfe quit his low whistling. "Followed you. The whole way south. Through mesas and fire zones. You think you had it tough? We had to do most of our driving and hiking after it was dark so the chopper wouldn't spot us. It was like Special Forces stuff. Jezebel's going to flip when she finds out she missed it."

True. I should be grateful. My friends hadn't given up on me when life got tough, and Jezebel hadn't come along for my rescue. If she had, I'd be sharing my limited floor space right now.

I shifted my body around the sets of legs and feet hogging my space. I pointed at Stone's and Melody's animal-skinned knees. "So? Your story? You two still haven't explained your mysterious reappearance. Rebecca and Wolfe being here makes some sort of sense. You being here is...impossible."

Melody paused mid-chew on a stick of something pungent with garlic. "What do you mean, Dove? Of course I had to come rescue you! I saw the cops take you away. And then when I told Stone, he said, 'Well, we'll just have to go get her out of jail.' And I was like, 'Yeah. Good idea. But where do you think they're keeping her?' And he said, 'Maybe that Wolfe guy will know since he's a Heathen, too.' And—"

"And long story short, they ended up at my doorstep in Sisters. For the record, I was a hundred percent supportive of their idea to bust you out of the detention center by force. But Rebecca, of course, talked us all out of it and sold us on this rescue-you-in-the-desert plan." Wolfe rubbed the back of his neck as if it was sore. "Which really, I don't think was much easier in the end. You ever camp next to a cactus, Dove? Unforgiving plants, cacti."

Big Brother Bender's silence filled the Jeep louder than Wolfe's chatter. So he'd decided to return to Mount Jefferson and then ran into Melody? I sucked my cheeks together to stop myself from demanding, *when did you decide to return, Stone? And why? Was it for Reed? The Council? For Melody?*

He caught my eye and glanced at the girl in the seat beside him. Then he stared out the open space next to him at the showers of falling stars in the deepening twilight.

I craned toward the Jeep's front. Rebecca and Wolfe could be typical sightseers with their dark glasses and Wolfe's electronic balanced on Rebecca's bare knees. They didn't react at all when an airplane flew over our dusty, empty road.

As the engine in the sky faded out, I pulled the flap of suffocating material off myself. "What about that light flashing on the cliff some nights? You must have noticed."

Melody giggled. She fiddled with Stone's bandage. "Us! That was us! We all hiked the cliffs those nights and waited for you, but only Stone knew the secret code. Right, Stone? He thought you'd recognize it. Did you feel less lonely knowing we were nearby? I figured you'd recognize my leather water pouch—"

"But, Melody, what about the bad—"

"—and know it was us." She didn't let me interrupt and ask about the poisoned water at the saguaro the night before the fire.

I tried again. "But that one time when the water

was bad—"

"And Stone saved you in the water? Well, he couldn't let you drown in the flashflood, could he? Although those two up front were mad at Stone. They thought he shouldn't have risked it. The hunters in the helicopter almost spotted him."

I made another attempt. "But when the water was poi—"

"We really cut it close, leaving you the pile of rats with that last water. Did you eat them? Stone said you would since you were skin and bones. And you found the compass to warn you to head southeast to catch the road? Well, I guess you didn't understand that message, since you headed the wrong way to that ghost town. But I wouldn't have understood the clue either, so don't feel bad."

I didn't feel bad. I felt frustrated. I clamped my lips tight while she chattered on without a breath about Lobo tracking them to their campsite last night, his questions, and how surprised she was. In that unique way she and I had of communicating, I understood her message.

Not now. Don't ask about the bad water now. Not safe. Later.

My pressed lips itched with the unspoken question. I reached under the tarp for my bag and felt around for Melody's possession. I dropped her worn, leather pouch onto her toes.

Fine. I'd wait. But once our time of private conversation came, she'd explain more about that poisoned water. And someone had splattered me with a bloody scent to bait a cougar. One of my rescuers must have seen something suspicious yesterday morning—if not Melody then one of the others. I'd start with Melody if she insisted.

And that fire, who'd set it?

A folded paper had wedged between my fingers when I'd fumbled for the pouch. Now I fingered it under the tarp. The familiar worn edges, the missing corner, the wavy, water-damaged paper. But Ruth's slanting scrawl hadn't faded. If I held it up to the Jeep's interior light, the others would be able to read it just fine.

A unanimous decision has been made for a spiritual conquest—note the change in the Reclaim from a physical to a spiritual nature.

Would my brother listen to me about the Reclaim without Gran there to speak, too? Would he believe Governor Ruth's note? Gilead might become so crazed about Gran's death that he'd take revenge on the unsaved in their territory despite it being a sin. Grandpa wasn't strong enough to stop him.

I sighed and eased the message back into my sock from where I'd removed it to bathe.

I'd been hiding the Council's missive so long, my mouth rebelled at blurting out the news as well as my role in delivering it. I could trust these four with the information, couldn't I?

I pictured Gran's wrinkled face showing new lines the last couple of nights at the campfire. She had carried the burden for both of us in secret until it had been my turn to bear it. It was still my turn. God would guide me, let me know who I should share the information with—and when.

I let my head fall back with a smack against Wolfe's chair back.

He reached next to where Rebecca dozed for something that rustled. A yellow, rumpled chip bag landed on my head.

There were only a few left since I'd devoured most of them earlier. I inhaled every last crumb, licking the salt from the foil, even though it stung my lips. "Water?"

Stone froze in reaching for a bottle from the stack behind him. Red and blue flashes bounced off the car's glass windows. Cops. He slid to the edge of his perch, ready to react, and I shifted to make room for his knees. Melody, who'd been using his good arm as a pillow, flopped over and resettled to doze.

I eased the tarp over myself. In my blindness, I heard the police car pull level with us. It passed by.

Something patted the tarp over my head. It must have been Wolfe's hand. "Breathe, Dove. They're watching the southern border for you tonight—not northern Texas. Don't you know that us Picketts got family in Mexico? They're on their way to pick you up at a crossing. At least Grandma's been hinting that to the authorities, last message she sent me. There's a manhunt for you down south. Got to feel bad for any skinny, blonde chicks vacationing in Cancun tonight."

24

Welcome to New Mexico.

~*~

You Are Leaving New Mexico—Hasta La Vista.

~*~

Now Entering Colorado.
Leaving Colorful Colorado.

~*~

Welcome to Utah, the Beehive State.
Utah Hopes You Come Again.

25

Now Entering Idaho.

I pointed at the map on Wolfe's electronic balanced on the Jeep's sloping expanse of white paint. "You're not taking us far enough west. No wonder this drive is taking forever. Look. Drive like that. Stop messing around."

My fingertip made an invisible line from the dot that represented us in Idaho all the way to the one marked *Prineville* in Oregon. I tapped the dot.

"Messing around?" Wolfe's scrunched nose approached the map. "But there's no road where you're pointing, Dove. Driving doesn't work that way. We can't move in a straight line."

"You say that. But you haven't even tried."

He threw up his hands. "Listen, I'm sorry. I'm sorry it's taken us six days—"

I held up two fingers. "You said I'd be home in two."

"I'm sorry you've had to share the floor of the Jeep with Melody." His dark brows pulled up in the middle as if he didn't lie. He was sorry about that.

Now that Stone had gotten sick, Melody claimed half the floor space for herself so he could stretch out in the whole back bench area—which was dumb since he had to half-sit, curled up in a ball and still lopped off.

"And I'm sorry the road builders around here are

morons."

"They are! Even my baby cousin Jovie can draw a better line with a stick while shutting her eyes. I bet even you could build a straighter road."

"Well that sweet compliment just earned you breakfast." He shoved away from the vehicle's nose and joined Rebecca for the short walk across the field toward the rundown structure labelled *Yummies Minimarket* at the edge of the highway. "Next time you get to explain roads to her, Becca."

"Little doughnuts! Don't forget." Doughnuts, with their silky outsides and crumbly sweet innards...my discovery of this delectable food was the best part of this eternal drive.

Rebecca gave me a weary nod and strode away. Melody trailed after her. "Orange drink, cheesy chips, those meaty bite things if they've got them..."

Rebecca's long legs sped up, creating space between herself and Melody. I wouldn't have minded more space between Melody and myself either since we'd been sitting on each other's feet for six days. But I wasn't allowed around any nonbelievers besides Wolfe since I was an escaped convict or something like that. So I stayed with the others, hidden behind the chicken farm where we'd parked.

"You ready to help me move him, Dove?"

I wandered to the other side of the Jeep to where Wolfe had helped Stone relocate for a break from the car. He slept propped up against the footing of a rusty, chicken feed silo. The guy weighed a couple hundred tons. Move him?

"Uh. I don't know, Melody. He seems OK—comfortable...enough..."

When he breathed, a strangled wheeze escaped.

Underneath his beard, his neck had to be bent funny.

"Oh, fine, fine, fine." I grabbed Stone's leg.

Together Melody and I pulled, grunted, and pulled again until his body slid down flat. The ash-brown head smacked the grass and bounced. His eyes popped open.

She clasped her pink cheeks. "Oops, sorry."

His lids slid down. "Thanks. Much...much better." A snore followed.

I paced back and forth in the damp, shin-high weeds, stretching my spine and inhaling the tainted morning air. But the poultry stink protected us since drivers sped up on smelly stretches of road. They didn't stop for doughnuts.

I swung my arms to get the blood flowing. "OK, Melody. Now that he's asleep and we're alone, you can explain about that water someone gave me in the desert that made my—"

"Shh. Our talking might wake him." She began to unwind the old shirt we used as a bandage from around his bulging muscles.

"—tongue go numb..."

The skin around the bullet hole was shiny red. Swollen. And I thought it smelled bad, although that might have been from the chickens.

I crouched down next to Melody, forgetting about the answers I'd been hounding her for, the ones she always had an excuse not to give me. I'd asked now out of habit, since I'd stopped obsessing about the whos and whys somewhere back in Utah.

My new reality had become the Jeep's scratchy floor, the hum of the engine, Melody's body lulling against my shins, the rip in the black chair back fluttering in the breeze, the odor of chips and chocolate. The previous two weeks of torturous desert survival had faded into a strange dream that didn't affect my future.

Funny how I'd yearned for Stone to come to me in Texas. I'd had six days of him traveling from state to state, mere inches away, and most of the time I'd forgotten he was there. He'd become part of the Jeep's seat. When he spoke, he was polite, but he never said more than five words at a time. The lips under the ashy beard never smiled or even frowned. His eyes avoided mine.

Stone Bender had become a boring guy.

He hadn't always been so dull. Did pain zap his personality? Sickness?

I poked the red skin with my finger, ignoring Melody's sharp intake and hand batting. The flesh was hot and tight. I prodded again. The muscles higher up in the arm contracted in a jerk and then relaxed.

I bit my lip. Someone needed to dig that bullet out. It might be infected. Did he have a fever? As I stretched a wavering palm at his forehead, a rooster crowed.

"In the car. Get in the car!" Wolfe and Rebecca hurried around the peeling-paint coop wearing their dark glasses. Their arms cradled promising food packages.

I shoved the dressing at Melody. "Wrap up his arm. Quick."

Wolfe tossed the doughnuts and chip bags in the vehicle's front area and tripped to a stop in front of the sprawled giant. "Oh man...Stone, Get up. We've got to go, dude. Fast. Jump in the car—"

"Wolfe, stop!" Melody flapped the stained cloth at him. "Why are you kicking an injured person? Stop kicking him!"

Rebecca shoved her aside. She confiscated the cloth and knotted it around the bullet wound. "He's not. He's waking him up, and you need to calm down. We all do. Everybody take a deep breath. In...and out..."

My lungs obeyed and expanded, whooshing away the whisper of panic. What was going on?

She slid under Stone's unbandaged arm. "Dove. Wolfe. Help me lift him. Stone, you're strong. You're going to stand and walk like a man to the car and climb in."

"Of course." Stone didn't open his eyes or move.

Wolfe squatted and grabbed his waist. I moved to his injured side. The Brae girl bounced anxious circles around us.

If only I could trade her for Jessica right now. Wait. No, that wasn't right. Trade a Christian for a nonbeliever? But I couldn't deny that though both girls were small and underfoot, Jessica was strong. She might even help.

Wolfe grunted and staggered under most of the giant's weight. "Next time someone wants to hitch a ride with me, I'm only saying yes if I can lift him. Or her—this includes girls, too, so listen up. Only humans I'm able to lift can ride in my Jeep. That's the rule. And the problem is we've been spotted."

I blinked and toppled onto the backseat. "Huh?" I squirmed out from under Stone's leg while he murmured an apology.

"We've been sighted. Specifically, you've been sighted, Dove. Seen and recognized. Not good."

Rebecca panted, leaning against the white paint and pinching the bridge of her nose above the dark lenses. "Wolfe just spoke with his grandma. The authorities don't believe her story that you're in Mexico. Someone spotted you in Utah. That's unfortunate for us. They figure you're heading back to Oregon."

My eyes widened, searching for the line of cop cars. But the only threat in sight was an aggressive rooster who strutted my way while pretending to search for bugs.

Still frozen next to the silo, Melody met my gaze.

No danger?

No danger.

Wolfe started the engine. "Seatbelts, everyone."

Instead of groaning at his worn joke, I curled up tighter on the fuzzy floor mat and patted my sock. It was such a routine, thoughtless gesture, I almost missed that nothing at my ankle rustled.

I patted my sock again and then shoved my hand inside the thin material. Then I ripped off my shoe. The paper was gone. *Gone.*

Like an out-of-control whirlwind, I searched the Jeep's floor, jamming my hands under Melody and toppling her. My feet stepped on and over her. I stumbled out of the vehicle onto the patchy weeds where I must have dropped Ruth's message.

With a burst of feathers, the rooster flapped out of my frenzied path. After my sixth circle around the Jeep and silo, I halted. My foot had grown icy in its soaked sock. I squeezed my eyes shut. My head leaned back until I looked at the puffy clouds.

I lost it—Ruth's message. Your message. I'm so sorry.

Shame weighed me down so I couldn't breathe. I'd never been eager to deliver that message from the Oregon Council to Rahab's Roof. I'd downright had a bad attitude. But now, now that I lost it, that message seemed the most crucial reason for me getting back to Oregon. How could I have been so careless with it in my sock? People didn't carry life-and-death missives in their socks.

God, why would You use such a brainless girl as me for Your messenger?

"Dove?" Rebecca's voice was extra careful, as if she addressed an unbalanced person.

I trudged over and climbed inside, ignoring the lifted glasses. I could only shake my head and curl up.

Melody offered me my shoe. She clicked the pink candy on a stick against her teeth. "You lose something, Dove? Can I help you find it? Was it something to eat?"

I hadn't yet told her—or any of them— about the message I was supposed to deliver. I'd never determined it to be the right moment to share that burden. I couldn't now. Not that I cared so much that they thought me a failure. God already knew.

But You love me even though I'm a mess?

More than you can fathom.

A wave of relief from my self-hate swept through me, drying the hot liquid in my eyes. My brain welcomed the reprieve but then bucked and threw the comfort off. An image formed, hazy turning solid. The picture stuck like a burr that wouldn't dislodge no matter how I struggled to pluck and toss it away.

A shadowed group wearing homespun clothes and animal skins crept through the night, whispering in Amhebran. In the starlight, the Christians' faces were fierce with that look my brother and dad wore. They approached a familiar, boxy home. One by one they dropped over the sill of the open window. From inside the home came a scream...

I swallowed my own strangled shriek and tried to shake the horror from my head. A real-life argument was going on around me. I let Rebecca's voice flow into my brain and displace the disturbing image of Wolfe with my brother's knife sticking out of his back.

"—hospital. Or at least an urgent care center. Stone, we can't take you home. If we do, you'll die from infection. You need real medicine and a doctor. A surgeon."

"You're wrong, Rebecca. You don't understand. Mum can fix me at home. She's a healer. That's what she does. She can fix me up...don't need a doctor." Stone's reply, longer than usual, was slurred with a ragged edge. Pain. I touched his hand, and his hot fingers clenched around mine.

Melody struggled to her knees among the candy wrappers and tumbled against me, breaking our grip.

Yes, Jessica would be better right now.

She patted the leather-clad forearm. "If we take him to nearby healers, won't they figure out he's a Christian? And what if they don't fix him when they find out? And what if they throw him in the detention center? And what if he dies...locked up?"

Wolfe snorted. "No way. No human beings would do that, lock him up if he has an infection and let him die...would they?"

The humming tires seemed loud for a few seconds.

Rebecca flipped her glasses down onto her nose. "It's worth the risk. He needs a medical professional who is experienced at removing bullets from infected wounds. He needs real medicine. Not chewed up herbs and tree bark. Dove, back me up."

I opened my mouth to agree.

Except...

I believed his mom could fix him. Unlike Wolfe and Rebecca, I'd grown up with God healing us through my aunt's chewed up herbs and tree bark. If Stone said his mom was a healer and could take care of him...well, then she could.

"Dove? Tell them you agree with me. That we'll drive him to a clinic."

My head bobbed at Rebecca's persistence, though I kept my lips clamped between my teeth. Why did I have to be the tie breaker? I wasn't sure of my vote.

Yesterday we'd passed two of those healing clinics Rebecca rooted for. When we passed the next clinic, if I agreed, then Wolfe would get Stone inside. Afterward, he would drive me home, and I'd be able to tell Gilead about the changed Reclaim decision. I'd finally share my burden that Grandma was gone forever...although, by now my family had to have suspicions that she wasn't fine and dandy. Did they believe we were both dead now? That belief would only make Gilead more vengeful come the fifteenth of May.

I needed to get home today—yesterday—which meant dropping Stone off at a clinic to be fixed up as soon as possible.

And Mount Washington, where Stone lived, would be an extra half-day drive out of my way. Not to mention his home was at the backdoor to Sisters, where the cops watched for me. They believed me to be Dove Pickett from Sisters. Taking Stone home to be healed would be a dangerous and dumb move.

Or...I could suggest Wolfe drive me home first...and let the rest of them deal with Stone.

My cheeks burned. Despicable. Selfish. Judas. I'd deserve all those names. Everyone in this car had done so much to help me. They'd hate me—and I wouldn't blame them—if I bailed out before we figured out how to help Stone.

Wolfe forced a weak laugh. "Dove? Don't ask me to haul this giant around a leafy forest full of nettles. Please."

Melody sniffed. "A bit clueless, aren't you, Wolfe? For your information, a fire took out most of the trees and brush at Mount Washington."

My cheeks began to cool. "She's right, Wolfe. Plus, the top of the mountain where he lives is pure rock. No trees."

For the first time, the Jeep swerved. "Up...the top of a mountain? No! Please, no."

I counted on my fingers. Five. I had five days left before the Reclaim. By dropping Stone off at a clinic, I could make it home and then to Rahab's Roof in time to stop the...

With a sickening lurch I remembered—all I had to do was get home.

I gulped. Heat radiated from Stone's swollen arm that dangled inches from my right ear. I took his hand in mine again.

Thanks to my brainless action of losing Ruth's paper, I could only stop one zealous Christian in Oregon from attacking—my brother Gilead. Two, if Micah Brae still hung around my property...and if he believed me.

I fought the image from before, the group of Christians with knives, who would someday soon die for their killing spree in Oregon. It faded, replaced by Stone in orange stripes. He was sprawled on a bench the color of fish guts, staring at a crack.

Was his arm healed? I couldn't tell. Maybe the people in uniforms would fix his arm before locking him up. Or not. Maybe they'd let him die of infection like Melody suggested, an easy way to get rid of a radical. He looked like one. We wouldn't be able to hide who he was.

What do You want, Lord? Tell me. I'll do it.

I uncurled and squirmed to my knees, throwing Melody and her cheese wrapper off of me. "Stone? Stone, if I say we take you home, you owe me. OK? And this is what I want in return. You're not going to fight in the Reclaim or let anyone else in your MTV fight. Ever." I gave his hand a shake.

Stone responded with a gust of breath.

"He's asleep, Dove. And what are you—"

"Melody, you remind him later what he agreed to. No hurting pagan people. My failure to deliver the Council's decision of peace isn't going to result in him killing unsaved people, against God's will."

I swiveled and stretched my torso between my two friends in the front. "Wolfe, you're taking Stone home. Yes, up Mount Washington, so don't whine and say you won't because you are. And then you're going to take me and Melody home—to my real home near Prineville—and drop off Rebecca, too. After that you'll head to Sisters, grab your sister and grandma, strap them into this Jeep, and you're going to drive yourselves across the Oregon border by the fourteenth. Promise to stay out of the state until...until things die down. Promise me."

I'd demanded they leave Oregon by the fourteenth and not the fifteenth. Some eager Oregon Christian might strike a day early, and the Picketts had to be somewhere out of danger if that happened.

"Wait. What? I'm...I'm—"

Slam. Rebecca's hand hit the Jeep's interior plastic

and cut through Wolfe's stutter of disbelief. "You didn't think I was going to keep Wolfe and his family safe, Dove? Of course I will! And what about me and my family? When exactly were you going to share with me the unimportant news of the Reclaim's changed decision of peace? After I slaughtered half of Portland?"

26

I repeated the message Ruth had entrusted to Gran and me.

Stone slept through it, and Wolfe and Melody didn't speak. But Rebecca's body radiated anger. Even her hair frizzled bushier. The veiling glasses she wore did nothing to hide her fury that I'd withheld the news of the changed Reclaim decision.

"And you didn't think to tell me you were the messenger?"

I shrugged. "I thought about it. It just wasn't...the time."

"Huh! Wolfe, hurry up and find an urgent care facility for Stone so we at least have that problem solved."

The driver glanced over his shoulder at me. His dark eyes, no longer laughing, found mine. I shook my head. *Ignore her*.

"Dove! Quit that. Wolfe, you know the smart thing to do. What would you do if it was Jezebel back there and not Stone? You'd do the only decent thing...drive us to a clinic. Think if it was Jezzy that was hurting. Or Dove. You'd want her fixed. You know what the decent thing to do is."

I tapped Wolfe's tense arm. "It's not...decent. She's wrong. Somehow, she's wrong. Wolfe, please. For me. Block her out. Plug your ears. Drive to Mount Washington."

I crushed my fingers into my ears to block them against Rebecca's next persuasive argument. A blast of thumping music vibrated through my body.

Wolfe gripped the wheel, focused straight ahead, and turned the music up even louder to drown out Rebecca, whose lips continued to move.

~*~

A few of her words must have leaked through the music. Wolfe managed to turn us around so we drove the same stretch of pavement through the pines six times while the sun set. It was night when we bumped to a stop in the groomed clearing in the national forest.

The music cut off. I rubbed my ears, filled with high-pitched ringing, and kicked the tarp all the way off. We'd made it to the gravel stretch near Stone's home. I attempted to catch a glimpse of Mount Washington's black sides against the charcoal sky.

How unreal to be back in this gravel clearing, the same one where I'd been forced into a stolen vehicle by the Benders last summer.

Rebecca broke the silence with her door slam. Outside in the moonlight, her full lips mashed into a line, and she made no move toward the back of the Jeep. She wasn't going to help with Stone. *Your decision—your problem*, her crossed arms declared.

Sky alive! Was this the first time she'd ever not gotten her way?

Rougher than necessary, I shook the other two awake. How had they slept through everything? I massaged my temples that still pounded with the music's beat.

Wolfe watched me in the mirror with raised eyebrows. "Please?"

"Yeah, Wolfe. We're helping Stone home—up the mountain. This is going to happen."

He slammed his door, too. But at least, unlike Rebecca, he came around to help me extract Stone onto the gravel.

The giant was still able to walk, but he wobbled like my grandma used to do in her stay-in-the-willow-chair days. Wolfe, myself, and Melody—whom I suspected didn't use much of her muscles—assisted him to the edge of the pebbles. We paused from panting. Stone panted the hardest.

Wolfe adjusted his grip on the leather tunic and craned his neck at the blackness above us. "Dove, when you say 'At the top of the mountain,' you don't mean the actual top—"

"Shish!" I slid out from under Stone's armpit and followed Rebecca's stunned gaze over to some blobs—juniper bushes.

Rebecca feared nothing. So why did she cower?

Melody's deer eyes mirrored her panic. *Danger.*

I felt the electric prickling now, too. Heard that whisper of warning in my gut. I'd almost missed it. I'd been too busy trying to haul the fainting giant to the clearing's edge.

A guttural growl rumbled from the hedges on our right.

"Darcy..." Stone became deadweight, so heavy I couldn't hold him. His body slowly crashed to the ground at our feet.

"S...Stone!"

His collapse jarred Melody out of her panic attack. She scrambled onto her knees beside him. "He's not...not..."

Wolfe bent over both of them. "Not breathing?"

"Not waking up."

I flicked my foot at both of them. "Shh."

A pair of reflective eyes glinted from the juniper, and a long, boulder-sized shadow detached itself from the vegetation. The monster bobcat paused in its slinking advance to issue a rusty yowl of warning.

"We're Stone's friends, Darcy." I reached down and cradled Stone's heavy, hot hand in mine. I lifted it to my cheek, catching a whiff of his blood. "Friends. Good, Darcy."

"Whatcha doing, Dove?" Wolfe's frozen stance betrayed he was stunned by the appearance of such a huge predator.

"Her name is Darcy. She's his pet, and she can sense a threat to her family. So don't act like a threat." I remembered Stone's shudder when telling me about his "family pet." And his disjointed stutter when describing her anger. I patted the unresponsive hand again. "Nice Darcy. We're friends."

Wolfe squatted next to Melody, who half-hugged Stone's chest. He ruffled the giant's long hair. Stone would've broken his hand if he'd been conscious. "Hey, buddy! Best buddy in the world. You're really a...a great guy, Stone. Really, really...great..."

Darcy slunk forward, ears flat.

Wolfe attempted a knuckle bump with the limp fingers. "It's not working! She's not leaving."

Rebecca spoke for the first time. "Because Stone looks dead, and you're messing with his corpse. Quit touching him. All of you."

Right away I saw what she meant. Both Wolfe and I skittered back, leaving Melody paralyzed against

Stone.

"Make it to the Jeep?" Wolfe whispered. "Dove? Rebecca?"

I spared a glance for the vehicle, ghostly in the twilight, and a five-second sprint from where I poised. I wasn't fast, but I was faster than...

"And let that beast get Melody? You know she's the slowest. That's just plain wrong." Rebecca shot Wolfe a glare Gilead would've approved. She began to inch forward, pupils fixed on Darcy's. "You're not going to attack, Darcy. Because I am not your enemy. We're not your enemies. You're not going to attack."

Sweat stung my eyes, but I didn't dare swipe at it or blink. Did her gift work on animals? I'd never asked.

With slowness that made a silent scream build in my throat, she eased Melody up off the giant's torso. "C'mon, Brae. Step with me. Another step. There you go. Good girl. Darcy, you stay there. Good girl."

Rebecca stopped when she reached us. Backing up further might cause Darcy to react, to treat us like prey. We huddled together. Someone swallowed. Someone else's breathing was too loud. Minutes passed.

Would we still be rooted here when morning dawned, held hostage by this wild animal with a vendetta? I couldn't take this waiting game.

I chin-gestured at Wolfe. "You. Jump on Darcy."

"What?"

"Shh. Like you did on that cougar in Texas." I didn't take my eyes off of the Benders' pet.

"Geesh, Dove. I had the element of surprise—"

"Then move fast..." I gave him a one-handed shove forward, "and surprise her."

My mistake because that small movement triggered the feline. She sprang.

Wolfe grabbed my wrist, and I glimpsed Rebecca crush Melody to her chest. Jezebel's brother whirled to face me with his back to the rushing animal. His damp forehead pressed against mine. Through the girls' screams, he exhaled the words, "I have to tell you, Dove, I love—"

"Darcy, *heel*!" An ear-piercing whistle hooked the cat midair. Four paws off the ground, she doubled back, black-tipped tail whipping against her bared teeth. She slunk off to stand next to the whistler, now a silent silhouette at the tree line.

I released my nails from the back of Wolfe's arm and squinted.

The stranger was a Christian. Bearded but not old. His bulky leather clothes couldn't hide his tiny build that seemed somehow familiar while his wide, haunting eyes took in our group.

I gestured at my old traveling partner for her attention. *Melody? Danger?*

She'd taken a few steps forward from our huddle, out of Rebecca's arms. Without a word, she crumpled in a faint next to Stone's unconscious body.

The stranger by the trees let out another shrill whistle, and Darcy disappeared into the woods at his back. He cocked his head to the side. Then he stepped around Stone without seeming to see him and approached Melody. He bent and poked the small, fur-covered torso.

"Mel?"

He threw his scruffy head back and laughed.

27

"No danger!" At the laughing stranger's call, a group of human figures detached themselves from the shadows at the forest's edge and trickled toward us. Unlike the guy crouching over Melody, they stopped at the Bender brother's prostrate form.

A man with a scar that ran all the way across his face fingered the bandage below Stone's ripped-off sleeve. "What happened to him, Zechariah? You crazy allowing them Heathen here? And why'd you go and send Darce off?"

Bearded faces turned toward me, and my tattooed-limbs sticking out from my borrowed clothes seemed to grow more visible in the darkness. I lifted my chin in defiance. Wolfe's arm came around me, but then he seemed to remember that I don't allow that kind of touching—not from him. He dropped his arm, but the rest of him stayed put so I could feel his heat at my back.

"Rebecca?" I needed my friend with the gift of words to explain who we were. She must make it clear that Stone had an infection. We hadn't done anything bad to him, so they couldn't blame us. "Rebecca?"

But she was scrambling after the first, small-framed stranger who'd carried Melody in the direction of the mountain's shadows. She stepped in his path to cut him off. Her fingers snapped and pointed at the ground.

"Put...the girl...down. You've absolutely no right to carry her off like this."

He halted in his action of obeying her. His shaggy head shook to clear away her words. "I don't? I'm her brother. That gives me the right, yeah?" He let out another odd ripple of merriment.

"Oh." Rebecca stepped aside with a frown. After a moment's hesitation, she followed him into the underbrush and disappeared.

A torch of anger flared inside of me. The stranger wasn't lying. He was Melody's older brother—Zech, she'd called him. Seven plus years ago, he'd been the Brae family messenger who'd traveled with my Uncle Saul to Mount Jefferson. He was the kid my uncle had thought he'd lost. The one he'd gone insane over trying to find.

I strode forward to catch up. This Brae would explain to me why he was here. I, Saul's niece, deserved that much.

A wall of leather-clad bodies with bearded, scowling faces blocked me. One shook his club at me. "Whoa, girl. Count yourself blessed—or lucky if you'd rather—that you are still able to walk away. Now walk. Before we change our minds. And take your filthy, smog spewing vehicle with you."

"She's not...I mean she's one of us, on our side. She's a Christian." Stone's soft voice split the wall apart. Each person turned to look at him lying on the ground and then back at me.

Wolfe jostled me when he threw up his arms. "Now he wakes up! Now. Not a minute ago, when his monster pet needed clarification on whether to eat us or not."

Erin Lorence

With the help of six men, Stone clambered to his feet. "H-hey, Dove. I guess I took a little rest...but where's Mel? Oh, hey...hey, best buddy." Between labored breaths, he raised a hand at Wolfe. He might as well have finished repeating all of Wolfe's gushing words since they hung in the air. *–best buddy in the world. Really a great guy...*

The breathing behind me hitched. "Now's the time he develops himself a sense of humor? If that bullet doesn't kill him, I will."

My elbow connected with Wolfe's ribs. These strangers outnumbered us. Two held clubs, and at least one clutched a spear.

Wolfe sighed in defeat. "Hey...buddy. Don't you worry...big buddy. I'll be right behind you. The whole way home."

~*~

The almost vertical hike up Mount Washington was unfamiliar in the darkness. We passed through one char-and-ash section, but other than that, the trees we wound through grew tall, their rippled bark free of fire damage.

Up ahead, something—or someone—fell with a rustling crash. I squinted up the slope.

"Sorry...don't know why...legs aren't working. Perhaps if I rest." Stone had failed at a climb over a fallen trunk a toddler could've made.

I paused at a spiky clump of mullein, letting the last of the MTV pass me until their remarks faded out of earshot.

"Who are these Heathen wannabes?"

"Stone trusts them, but they drive?"

"If my girl wore indecent clothes like that I'd..."

Wolfe snagged my backpack, keeping me in the waist-high weeds. "Life. I love life. Down there, when it looked like some of us were going to die, I realized how much I didn't want to. Life suddenly looked pretty good. So I'm explaining to you, in case you were wondering what I was trying to say before. It's life I love, all right? Stop obsessing over it."

Moving as fast as he spoke, his lips bumped my cheek.

I staggered back, grabbing the torch-like plants to regain balance. "Hey!"

He darted forward. Voices exclaimed when he shoved past. Higher up the slope his tall figure became a leaning post for Stone's taller form.

What *had* Wolfe said in the clearing? I'd been focused on the cat's trajectory and whose face she was likely to rip off first.

He'd shouted. He'd shouted something about loving...life?

My skin warmed in the high elevation air. But it'd be dumb for me to march after him and call him out on his lie. It'd be almost as dumb as Wolfe having said aloud what he'd started to say when Darcy attacked— and for having done what he just did.

But I owed Wolfe. Big time. He'd jumped on a cougar for me. He'd gotten me out of Texas, driven me to Oregon, and kept me supplied with doughnuts along the way. Yeah, I owed him...although not enough to let him touch my face like that again. I hunched a shoulder and scrubbed the cool spot with my sleeve.

My repayment?

Because I owed him so much, I'd forget about what he'd done just now and what he'd said—and what he'd meant when he'd said it, a love beyond friendship. And I'd never think about him loving whoever...whatever...again.

You're welcome, Wolfe.

28

My torso flopped onto the last rocky ledge at the top of the mountain. I let my legs dangle a moment in space before I heaved them up.

Was this the place? Home sweet home for Stone?

A brown bat dipped toward me in a kamikaze move. I rolled aside, watching his fluttering form fall below the ridge until he disappeared into the gloom. I lay at the edge of a cold, dreary, barren quarryland. As I rubbed the sweat drying on my goose-bumped arms, the odor of ancient smoke and moss rose into my nostrils—a nose-wrinkling vapor from the dank rocks under my soles.

A thud echoed, as if someone shifted rocks near the mountain's peak. Yards away, the pointed, gray mass reared up. I clambered to my feet and pivoted a full circle.

What? There wasn't a *Go Away* sign stuck in the bedrock?

The villagers of this MTV did not want or need me here on Mount Washington. They'd carried their wounded friend up the mountain without any help from me. Stone's mom would heal him, also without help from me. And yet I'd tagged after the others, pretending I was needed like a pet dog. Wasting precious time.

I gasped. The Enemy's plan was so clear in the light of the cold morning. So simple. How had I not recognized his scheme? Satan was using my worldly relationships to jeopardize my mission...at least the part I could still finish. How could I be so brainless?

I scrambled to the outcropping's edge to begin my solo climb down to the Jeep. Rebecca, Wolfe, and Melody, when she woke, would miss me at some point and follow. And if they didn't, I'd find my own way home. I'd stuck around for Stone, so no one would hate me for leaving.

A songbird whistled at my back, and I turned.

A single, ash-gray dove fluttered toward a pile of rocks framing a cave entrance in the side of the mountain. As it settled, a slice of orange sunbeam struck. The sunrise's glow spread, flooding the whole depressing landscape into warm brilliance. The dove cooed, as if glad to be there. An invitation?

God? Do I...?

I stepped away from the bat's path and wandered into the pool of light. The knot in my gut dissolved. I tilted my head back and stretched my arms wide, soaking up its heat.

Another three-note whistle wavered. Near the cave's opening, Wolfe, lips pursed, beckoned me to join him.

At my approach, he grinned and patted a vacant boulder bathed in the golden light. Bearded males in head-to-toe leather occupied the rest of the chopped-out stone chunks arranged in a sloppy circle around a stone oven. They'd stopped their grumbling to eat with Zech nearest the oven.

I peered around, and the catch between my shoulder blades loosened. Darcy wasn't with them. But neither was Stone, Rebecca, or Melody.

My body wilted into a comfortable divot in the

worn granite. My chilled skin tingled in the puddle of sunlight until I shuddered.

"I love venison. Love, love it." Wolfe crammed a brown cord of it into his bulging mouth. "Do you love it, Zech?"

Melody's brother fixed his gaze on Wolfe.

Wolfe didn't seem to mind the guy's unblinking, crazy eyes...or when a villager got up and wandered away in disgust.

I half-rose too. Wolfe seemed unable to shut up, jittery with a need to chatter. But the warmth kept me sitting. I gnawed at my venison, surveying Zech, and *not* counting the number of times Jezebel's brother managed to work the word "love" into his jabberings.

He said "love" seventeen times.

He ran out of things to comment on about the time the oven ran out of food. In the merciful pause, I leaned forward. "Brae? There are some things you should know. You ruined Melody's life when—"

Wolfe's whistling cut through my accusation. It was a simple, Christian, kid's tune. "Jesus loves me, this I know..." Wolfe's eyes smiled into mine while he filled the smoky air with his music.

How'd he even know that song about Jesus?

I flung my uneaten venison piece back into the open oven and abandoned my perch that cradled my body almost as well as a hammock. I plunged into the cave's gloom. Behind me, Melody's brother's voice joined in with Wolfe's chorus. "Yes, Jesus loves me. Yes—"

After a few blinks, my vision adjusted. The cavern I hesitated in stretched longer than wide...although, the back of the cave disappeared into inky blackness, so who really knew? Above my head the ceiling reached a mile high, touching the sun. Splotches of the morning rays dazzled down through cracks and spotlighted rock and homey objects that didn't belong in a cave.

A group of people, including Melody, kneeled in the largest sunspot around someone lying on the ground. I picked my way toward them, through the collage of shadows and light illuminating whittled cooking utensils that dangled from crevices. An iron pot big enough for a deer to curl up in hung from a medieval chain. I stuck my head over its black side. Empty.

My feet stumbled in their hurry to get past what I guessed to be the village's arsenal—spears, knives, iron traps with spikes, and boxes with wires that looked like what Gilead used to electrify our zip lines.

A cold moisture drizzled down my spine by the time I reached the sunbeam where Mrs. Bender sweated over her son. Stone's face glowed bone-white against the dark blanket spread underneath him.

I crouched too and grunted my approval at the slop of leaves she pressed against the red skin she'd already smeared with green paste. At his waist level, Melody leaned away from the messy bullet on the edge of the blanket. Her mouth twisted like she might be sick.

I rescued Stone's hand from the danger.

His lids opened at my cool touch then slid down again. An etched line between his bleached brows disappeared, reappearing at the sound of feet moving closer. His fingers convulsed around mine.

Mrs. Bender's hazel eyes glanced from me, to Melody, to Zech, whose shadow blocked some of our light. She smoothed Stone's clinging hair back from his forehead and then swiped at her own ashen-blonde strands that escaped her bun.

She stood and gathered the bloody debris. "He'll get better I think. When he rests." Though her face and wiry body represented an older, female Reed, her soft tone was all Stone.

"He will. I mean...we'll let him. Rest. I promise." Melody's gaze devoured the small mother. Was she remembering her own? Or realizing that this lady could've been hers too if she'd stayed in her courtship with Reed? Although marrying Reed wouldn't be the only way to have her as a mother-in-law. Had that thought passed through her mind, too?

Zech claimed Melody's hand, settling with it on the floor beside her. She curled up on herself, chin against knees. "Hey."

"Hey."

I waited another five seconds. Then I exploded. "That's it? Melody, you've thought him dead for seven years, and you're not kicking him in the teeth that he's not? Zechariah, you don't know me but—"

"You're Saul Strong's kid."

"Ha! Wrong. He's my uncle, and not that you care, but he thinks something terrible happened to you, too. Do you know how many lives you've trashed by not returning home? I don't know what selfish, idiotic idea kept you staying here without a word to anyone back home who cares...but can't you pull together enough brain cells now to understand that your sister deserves more than a 'hey'? Unless she already had it out with you while you two hiked here?"

I could tell by Melody's soothing rocking she hadn't demanded answers.

Before I could continue my accusation, Stone whipped his hand out of mine. He covered his eyes.

"Melody, Dove's right. I should've...should've told you. I knew. Reed and I knew the second we met you who you were. He told me not to tell you that your brother lived with the MTV because...because you'd leave him. Us."

Zech peered into his sister's face with that fixed, owl-eyed expression that I hadn't yet seen shift to anything more human. "Have you ever realized you've been dead, Mel? I've been dead. Been buried in the ground more than half my life in that place we called home. The day I became messenger was my birth, and I swore to myself I'd never be buried again—not alive. And never by choice."

I'd reclaimed Stone's fingers. Now I relaxed my brutal grip. "Why'd you let my uncle think you'd gotten lost on your journey together to the Council?"

His unblinking stare shifted to me. "Saul Strong? He promised my dad he'd bring me home. I heard him, the night before my birth. He was going to keep his promise."

"Of course he would have. He doesn't lie. But how did you escape—I mean ditch—him?"

"Satan's workers attacked us." He stared at a spot past my left ear, smiling as if reliving a pleasant dream instead of what any sane Christian would recognize as a nightmarish memory. "Their attack allowed me to escape your uncle while he stayed unconscious. But I realized I couldn't go to the Council. He'd wake up and search for me there and force me home. He could've made me too. Saul was—"

Wolfe settled next to me. "Fierce? Intense? Slightly scary, while never giving a thought for others' opinions? It's a Strong family trait. His niece has it, too. After a while you get used to it...and even come to like it. Until eventually you wonder why everyone else in the world is so boring, and you know that to live without seeing that Strong every day would be unbearable."

I caught my breath at his implied apology. He reached over and took my other hand.

I freed myself from both guys' hands and crossed my arms.

Zech shook his head. "When I left Saul, I wandered with no idea where to go except to find somewhere to hide. How could I know what to do? My parents had taught me nothing useful. I was a newborn baby in the world, alone...until Reed found me. He kept me alive and away from Saul. He taught me. He became my brother. I'm sorry, sister, but I'm a Bender now, not a Brae. My new family showed me how to use my gift instead of wasting it."

"Gift?" Wolfe shoved his fists into his pockets. "Another Christian with a gift? Don't tell me you've got one too?"

I continued to glare at Zech. "Why do you think he, Darcy, and half their village waited for us at the bottom of the mountain last night? That's his gift. The ability to know—to see—more than most of us. But he only sees what God allows. So Zech, did God show you traumatizing your family and abandoning my uncle during your journey a few years back? Or was that your own idea?"

Inside the dark beard, the Brae teeth flashed again—but not in the way Wolfe's sometimes did that made my own lips want to twitch up. "We're moles, Dove. That's what other Christians call the type of family I was born into. Moles. Do you understand being a mole? Hiding under the ground? Blind and existing on worms?"

"Of course she can't. Because she's a bird." Rebecca's voice resonated from the cave's inky shadows. She tottered toward us into the light, her hands out as if she'd just woken from a nap. "And Stone is a bat while I'm a city rat. Moles, birds, bats, rats. Underground Christians, tree-dwelling Christians, cave Christians, city Christians. They're only names for us, not excuses for us to sin or to act inhuman. Let's cut out the excuses for our actions, shall we?"

"Arrrrgh!"

At Stone's cry, his mom knelt, patting for his pulse.

"No, mom. It's not...pain here. It's here." He touched his temple, then his chest. "I can't take the agony—the secret's crushing me. Melody, I can't keep it to myself anymore. You can't either. No more excuses, like Rebecca said. We can't hide the secret, not even for Reed."

He heaved himself onto his good elbow, ignoring his mom's gentle attempt to push him down. His light irises bored into mine. "Dove, your lost message to Rahab's Roof is in Melody's satchel. I put it there...just like I was the one who tried to stop you in Texas. Me and Melody, we're the ones who almost killed you in the desert."

He flopped back down as Wolfe's fist smashed him in the face.

29

"Stone!" With a shriek, Melody flung herself over his unconscious form, knocking against Wolfe, who shook out his bruised knuckles.

Rebecca lost her calm. Leaning around Mrs. Bender, who mopped the new gash on Stone's cheekbone, she ranted at Wolfe for knocking him out. Then she rounded on Melody. "You tried to hurt Dove? Explain."

Unnoticed by everyone—except maybe Zech who contemplated the sunlit hole overhead while humming "Jesus Loves Me"—I ruffled through Melody's bag in the shadows. My fingers tightened around a familiar paper. With a glance at the dog-eared, folded letter, I shoved Governor Ruth's message into my own pack.

Melody's tearful plea slowed my feet at the cave's entrance. "I'm sorry, Dove. We're both sorry, but what choice did we have?"

I pivoted.

She wilted under my glare and flung a scared side-glance at Rebecca's fists on her hips. "After you abandoned me and I was lost in the woods, alone—"

I charged forward to shake her but stopped short and took a shaky breath. "I did not abandon you in the Mount Jefferson wilderness! I was arrested. By people with weapons. But let me guess. Reed found you?"

"Oh, yes! So you see, when he rescued me, I

realized what an idiot I'd been. I need him. I love him, and he wants to marry me. He says he's forgiven how much I wounded him when I left. He says he'll believe that I love him if I join him in his mission. My part is to stop you from reaching Portland. It's God's will you be stopped, and Reed was desperate to do it and couldn't. And he needed me. So I helped. But that doesn't mean I don't like you, Dove. I do. It's not personal."

I had underestimated Reed. Both in his influence over Melody and in his speed in finding out about the changed Reclaim decision, and that I was Ruth's messenger.

Governor Ruth must have shared the news too soon with leaders at Mount Jefferson, which included Reed. Had he killed her, another old lady like my grandma standing in the way of his war? I had assumed she still lived since I hadn't been charged with her murder.

I swallowed hard. "And Stone? Why did he decide to take part in Reed's mission? You told me before Stone had left his brother behind and went home."

She glanced at the giant's unresponsive form for help. "Uh. That's the reason—Reed is his brother. Going against his brother tore him apart. He said he made it halfway to the MTV and then couldn't take the guilt. Reed said he'd forgive him too if—"

"If he stopped me from reaching Portland."

Unexplained struggles of my desert-wandering began to click together into understanding. Someone had tried to help me...and at other times tried to hurt me. Rebecca and Wolfe's presence had kept Stone's and Melody's sabotage in check. Together, the four had tried to help me—with lifesaving water, rats to eat, and a planted compass to alert me to which direction I needed to travel. But there must have been times when Melody and Stone sneaked away from the others.

I pointed at Melody's worn satchel. "The poisoned water in your leather pouch. You and Stone planted it for me."

"Poisoned water?" Rebecca's fists raised from her hips.

"You...he tried to poison Dove?" Wolfe lurched forward but stopped when Stone's mother shielded her son's head with her thin arms.

Stone was awake. His guilty expression evaporated as his lips moved. "I had to stop you, Dove. But I couldn't let you die. Remember? I didn't let you die."

"I remember, Stone. You saved me from drowning. But then you offered me poison and lit a wildfire at my heels."

Melody sat up straighter. "But not to kill you! I promise. The helicopter people—the people Rebecca knew—would have saved you before the smoke and flames hurt you. And the water I left wasn't poisoned. I only mixed it with ground-up toadstools to make you sleep for a while, so they'd take you back to the detention center instead of setting you free to go to the place in Portland where God doesn't want you. Dove, you need to listen. Listen to Reed. Don't go to Portland. It's not right!"

I grabbed Wolfe's elbow to hold him back from doing violence. "And the last days in the desert, Melody? Turning me into cougar catnip?"

Zech clapped, a slow round of applause that echoed.

"Oh, Stone." The woman frowned her reprimand at her son. "My recipe? You used my concoction to terrorize this girl with a wild animal?"

"I didn't want to. It was only a precaution, and Reed demanded...but the cat didn't kill her. I wouldn't have let it." Stone shifted his face out of the sunbeam and into the shadows.

"So, you two never came to Texas to help me survive or escape. You tagged along to make sure Wolfe and Rebecca failed." I yelped at an unexpected wet touch on my forearm and skittered away from Darcy's exploring nose. She appeared even bigger indoors.

A bearded stranger jogged a detour around the animal and saluted Zechariah who continued to mouth "cougar...catnip."

"Sir. Sir, there are Heathen in the lower quarter near the road, advancing north."

Melody's brother's owl-stare didn't shift from the overhead patch of sky. "Yes. Of course. I was right. Alert the MTV of our lockdown. Everyone's to make shelter in the cave. No more chats or songs now. I'm focusing on our outcome for survival." He rapped his skull with his knuckles and settled down as if to sleep.

~*~

I picked my way between groups of sleeping families. A woman swatted at me in her sleep when I mistook her hair for the shaggy mat I thought safe to step on. I froze, but she didn't wake. Behind me, Wolfe grabbed my backpack as if tottering on one foot and unable to set the other down.

A tall, bushy-haired silhouette at the cave's entrance waved at us from the solitary lamp's light. An impatient gesture. "Hurry up."

Wolfe released my belongings and prodded me. "You should hurry up."

I bit back my retort about weak minds and advanced forward until I could peek around Rebecca's square shoulder at the barren, moonlit landscape. My tense body relaxed. No Darcy.

A human figure detached itself from the misshapen oven surrounded by boulders. "One. Two. Three of you."

Panic coursed through me, but Rebecca's quick intake of breath was the only sign her calm faltered. With a wide, crooked smile, she thrust out a hand for him to shake. "Zech. I'm glad we have a chance to thank you before we take off. We appreciate your hospitality, sheltering us the last two days—"

I snorted. I would have said "imprisoning us" and I wouldn't have thanked him either. Darcy paced the cave entrance from dawn until midnight, which was the reason we sneaked out during the wee-morning hours in the cover of darkness.

Rebecca's foot shot backward at my shin. "But Zech, you must agree it is time for the three of us visitors to leave. We're draining your limited resources and taking up more space than we're worth—plus we make the villagers uncomfortable. It's not fair to ask them to share with us more than they already have when they are suspicious of our loyalties to God. Of course, Melody will stay with you. We wouldn't dream of asking her to leave after being so recently united with you, her older brother she's missed all these years."

I leaned around Rebecca. "Keep Stone, too. Please. We don't want him." Somewhere behind me the traitors slept. When I'd last seen them, Melody lay curled up inches away from a fast-healing Stone, their fingers entwined.

As if to distract me from the tightening in my gut, Wolfe grasped my backpack. He used it to sway me back and forth in a rocking motion. *Let it go. Let it go. Let it go.*

The sole of Rebecca's shoe knocked my leg again while I batted at my pack. Only Zech remained motionless, continuing to block our path.

In the pause that dragged, Wolfe quit fiddling with my bag. He put his mouth to my ear. "You think her magic power of words won't work on this guy."

"Because his brain's not right?" I broke off my whisper to sidestep our gifted speaker's kick. "You think being nuts blocks Rebecca's ability to convince him—?"

"Leaving...is unsafe." Zech had turned and faced the edge of the ledge beyond the oven. "The godless are still down there. At the bottom of our home. Searching."

Wolfe jostled me aside to stand toe-to-toe with Zech. "I'm a godless. So what? If park rangers ask us, we're just normal, non-fanatical hikers who got lost. No crime in that. As everyone in this cave knows, we look the part, right? And the rangers are hunting for us down there because of my Jeep. If I leave it parked down there much longer, they're going to tow it, which I don't exactly have the funds to extract legally—"

"Only someone more than nuts would move your vehicle. I wouldn't worry about losing it."

A burst of need washed over me. *Three days.* Only three days until the Reclaim. "Let us go, Zech."

He continued to block us with his vague

expression. Then he shifted aside, and Wolfe and I sprinted for freedom

Only Rebecca paused. "Tell us our outcome, Zech? God gifts you with knowledge, and we'd appreciate you sharing with us what He's shown you—if He's shown you."

Melody's brother rapped his skull. He mimed locking his lips and tossing the invisible key over the edge of the rocky clearing where Wolfe and I poised, ready to slide down the scree onto the crags below.

~*~

I raced the moon, as it lowered behind us, and then the rising sun. The bright orb gripped the blackness to the east, washing it to charcoal. Precious moments of the three days I had left to find the unknown radio station and reach home—not necessarily in that order—slipped away.

I plunged down from the last crag onto a pile of ash between charred stumps. *Hurry, hurry, hurry...*

The birds had awakened for their pre-dawn clamor when we moved from charcoaled nature to lush nettles and brush that sprang back when stepped on. Fir branches up ahead rustled.

"Get back over here, Wolfe! You too, Rebecca. Stop being wimps. It's raccoons or opossums. Not a bear."

Further down the slope, the vehicle appeared ghost-like and motionless between an opening in the last line of evergreen branches. I let out a shaky laugh. Our ride hadn't been stolen or moved. Something Zech had said earlier had been poking at me. *Only someone more than nuts would move your vehicle.* I gripped the rough trunk of a pine and stepped around it.

A beam brighter than a flashlight's blasted me.

"Dove!" Someone yanked my arm, but I fell forward, too blinded to see the tripping roots at my toes. I landed on all fours.

"Freeze! Stop moving!"

At the click of a weapon, I quit scrambling backward. I squinted at the uniformed figures spread out in the gravel clearing below me. A familiar figure leaned against the Jeep's white side.

No! I slammed my scratched-up palm against the bracken.

Savannah shoved up. "Hello, Dove."

Had another so-called friend betrayed me, Melody and Stone style? Had someone I trusted led me into this trap? I spared a backward glance.

Rebecca had vanished, leaving Wolfe and I behind to cringe into the light. Then, louder than the shock on Wolfe's face, a stick snapped. A raspy grating of rubbed twigs started up from yards away, as if a signal for my attention.

I skimmed the columns of trees behind us. A leather-clad arm moved from behind one. Zech Brae stood, flattened against the trunk but well camouflaged. Out of sight of the cops. Darcy skulked in the bushes at his knee.

My fingers flexed into claws until I clenched handfuls of dirt and dead needles. "What?"

He released the twigs and smoothed his pet's hackles, pulling her against his leather pants so the hunters below wouldn't see her. His whisper held laughter. "You had to be captured, Dove. Had to. Because Melody says Reed doesn't want you to reach Portland. And you never agreed you wouldn't go.

Shalom."

With a brief salute, he slipped away.

Heavy feet tromped up the slope. A cop fastened a plastic strap around my wrists and pulled me to my feet beside Wolfe.

30

Complicated sentences swirled around me like fog. The fake wood tabletop under my elbows beckoned me to lay my head on its smooth coolness. Whatever needed to happen would happen while I hid my face under my shortsleeved, orange-clad arms. Rebecca's elbow knocked against mine. I jerked up straighter in my metal chair.

"...will be able to argue that at her arraignment..." Blah, blah, blah...legal stuff that made no sense.

Lucky Wolfe. At this minute, he'd be cozy and asleep in his home. Rebecca had shown up here at the CTDC. My cheeks burned that I'd suspected her of betrayal. She had gotten all the charges against him dropped, and she and I sat shoulder-to-shoulder now in this detention center to fight for my freedom.

I gazed glassy-eyed at Prosecutor, the pagan stranger next to Savannah, who aimed another question at me. Rebecca deflected it. With a swift counterattack, she argued I had fulfilled the terms of my agreement, since I'd reached civilization in Shafter, Texas.

She waved a confident finger at a map of the nation stuck on the pastel wall. "Civilization. The society, culture, and way of life of a particular area. There are to date six known residents of Shafter who live according to the culture of that town. Dove encountered at least one resident. Civilization."

My brow wrinkled. A grizzled creature in overalls had tried to shoot me off my escape bicycle seconds before Lobo had tackled him. Was the shooter the resident and civilization? Was my case so desperate Rebecca declared that? My heart sank to my stomach, and my head inched toward the tabletop. Even with her gift, this argument would crumble to less than termite dust.

The metallic door swung open. A dark, handsome man strutted into our room, grinning. He grabbed a chair from the wall, turned it backwards, plunked it down next to Savannah's, and straddled it.

I jumped up."Lobo? Lobo! What are you doing here?"

Savannah snapped her fingers at my outburst. "Sit. Lobo is joining us since he's the executive producer of *Fanatic Surviving*, and the outcome of your future concerns him and his show."

Rebecca translated for me under her breath. "She means he's second in command of the television show. He's in charge of it, like a boss."

This piece of unfathomable information wedged itself into my brain with a painful throb. "But you...you lied to me, Lobo. You told me—"

"I didn't lie, terrorista Dove Pickett. Maybe I didn't tell you every single detail about my life...but never do I lie."

My empty chair jerked forward and hit the back of my knees, forcing me to sit. Rebecca plunged back into her argument about the civilization I'd reached, fulfilling the terms of my agreement. Lobo's smile grew.

He appeared healthy enough, except for some

shadows under his eyes. And his cheekbones jutted out more than they had above his stubble. I had wasted hours in the Jeep, gnawing my thumbnail that he'd been hurt or punished for helping me.

Now consumed with the news that Lobo wasn't who I thought he was, I allowed my mind to glide over the surreal events of my last days of desert survival.

When I'd called it quits in Shafter, Lobo had commanded me to find a road. According to Jessica, he'd broken rules telling me about this. Rules he'd helped create? Hmm. And afterward, he'd tossed me up to the roof and into Stone's arms so I could escape Savannah and the consequences of my failure. Later, Melody had said something about Lobo finding them in the hills the last night...with questions.

I leaned forward, interrupting someone who shushed me. "You remember what my God did, Lobo? In the desert?"

His wiry body copied my tilted posture. "Yes. I remember you telling me a nice story about your God battling Satan. But don't let my pity for your circumstances fool you. Your God...He is nothing. Only a figment of your mind and a fib your parents taught you."

He spoke in the same blustering tone he had when he'd lied to Jessica up on the cliff about the helicopter circling to find a better spot to land. And when he'd told us that the fire wouldn't burn where we stood.

I cocked my head to the side. "So why can't you sleep anymore? You stay awake remembering those miracles. You want to believe what you saw. You felt Him. Your heart believes in Him, even if your brain won't."

Across the table, his dark face blanched while

Savannah's steamed up red. Her voice was a like a viper's hiss. "Ms. Pickett, if you continue to interrupt and harass in this disrespectful manner, you will forfeit your right to be present—"

Lobo waved her down. "No, she stays. Only remember we're not here because of me, terrorista Pickett. You broke the terms of *Fanatic Surviving*'s agreement and caused a breach of contract."

Rebecca flung herself into this new argument. "Terms which you aided her in breaking. If you don't lie, then you can't deny it. You helped her. There are witnesses."

My hands covered my ears, blocking their back-and-forths so I could make out the low voice of truth trying to get my attention. A surge of understanding broke over me, followed by a scary realization that made my palms sweat. I lowered them. "Stop talking, Rebecca. Listen. It's me they want. Lobo—and Lobo's boss—they want me. Because I can make or break their show.

"That's why I've been hunted so hard. I showed you, Lobo, what no other religious contestant has before. No one has faced so many disasters and struggles...or conquered them like I did as a Christian. What my God did—saving me from plagues, flood, and fire—amazes you. You want to give the television watchers more miracles. *Fanatic Surviving* wants more of me on their show. No. They want me to be their show. Every time.

"Rebecca, after I stand trial—and lose—they plan to bargain with me like last time. I'll survive two weeks in whatever environment they choose. In exchange, I'm given a chance to win my freedom. But I won't. They'll set it up so I can't, just like before in the southwest. I'll be trapped in a doomed cycle forever."

In the resulting silence, even Savannah traded her sneer for a dropped jaw. Lobo, tilting forward on his chair legs, lost his balance. His chair toppled with a crash, leaving him standing. Prosecutor stood and without a word, walked out of the room.

Rebecca crossed her arms. "You want Dove? OK. You drop all charges against her today, and we'll agree you can have her for your show in the future. But she is a free woman and has a say in the where and the when of the filming. And if you choose to use the footage you shot—"

"They've already shown it. At least part of it." As soon as I blurted this unfounded fact, I recognized it was true. "They've shown the world what God did for me in the Texan wasteland, and the godless won't leave them alone. They want to know more, and they think I'm the key to finding out."

Rebecca's lopsided smirk announced our victory. "Dove is known now. And she will use the fame you unwittingly gave her to either make or break your show. So? You decide."

Lobo stuck out his hand. "I accept your terms. We film your next survival July fifth."

I hesitated. Shaking meant more torturous treks with the hostile crew and facing their cameras. I could never go back to hiding from nonbelievers and the confusing connection I felt with them...because they'd know me. If I agreed, I was giving myself to the Enemy's people, allowing millions of them to watch my movements and my interaction with God. They would see my nonviolence. My faith. Recognize my name. Christians like Reed would call me a traitor or worse. Satan's helper.

I grasped Lobo's hand and shook.

His other callused hand came around mine, trapping it. "Of course you agree. You kept your eyes on the door, waiting for Jessica to appear when I came in. You miss your little friend, terrorista Dove. Don't fret. I'm the boss. I can guarantee she's on the team for next time. I will convince her daddy."

"But I don't...I don't miss her...a nonbeliever."

"Pickett from Sisters, yes? Then I am confident you will renew your friendship even before July."

31

A cop car almost mowed me down when I fled from the CTDC into the middle of the paved parking lot. It flashed its lights at me.

"Excuse her, Officer. She was born blind and still hasn't adjusted. Get in, Dove."

I scrambled into the Jeep that'd pulled around and now idled level with me. Wolfe grinned and handed me a skinny box of doughnuts.

I fiddled with the cardboard top. "Today's May the fourteenth."

"You're welcome, Dove. Yes, I'm fine since the detention center was a blast. And, yep, the fourteenth, still two weeks until my birthday—plenty of shopping time."

Tomorrow was the Reclaim. Tonight at midnight, it began. I studied the glowing clock.

He eased us forward, in the direction of a road with painted lines. "So...to your home then, Dove? To stop your brother from hacking people up and in all likelihood getting himself killed in the process?"

I nodded. "No. Wait!"

We lurched to a stop. He waved at the police car following us to go around. "Not home?"

"How long to get us to Portland?"

"I'd say three hours or so."

My fingertip strained against the plastic window glued to the cardboard on my lap until the clear film broke. I pinched the doughnut's brown, crumbly coating.

He leaned out his window. "Just go around already, sir. Fine!"

With an engine rev, he bumped us onto the road. "Where are we heading, Dove? I'd take you to Portland except you're dying to get home first."

"I never said—"

"I know you. You want to get to your family."

The cardboard bent. My fingers pressed the chunks into smaller crumbs. How had this happened? How had I gotten so close to this nonbeliever that he knew my brain? Since Texas, I'd accepted his ever-presence without examining reasons. Situations beyond myself had jammed us together. Like a squirrel and a mouse forced by a violent storm to share a burrow.

But now, he'd popped into my life again of his own free will. I hadn't asked him to meet me at the CTDC. How had he even known I was leaving today? And again, he fell into my plans, as if my plans were his.

From my peripheral view, the afternoon sun lit up his carefree face. *Why are you here, Wolfe?* But what if I asked, and he realized he didn't have a decent explanation? Worse, what if I didn't want to hear his explanation? I sensed it in the offing. Too intimate. Too full of declarations. No, better not ask.

I lowered my lids. The sunlit red pressed down. "Of course I want to get home. But..."

But I couldn't.

I gave up fighting the truth. My journey must follow the course of my dream with the red I'd dreamed so many weeks before. I'd already reached the desert, but I still had one more stop to make—my next stop. I had to find the columns of gray cement. No matter how I wished it, the gray columns were not trees near Prineville. They were buildings in a city. Portland. Rahab's Roof.

I flung out one last question, all my hope hinging on his response. "Can we drive to Portland and still reach my home before midnight?"

He exhaled in a whistle. "Depends. Do you have the address of where in Portland?"

I shook my head.

"A phone number? A clue about the building or landmark near where you need to be?"

I tossed the ruined box onto the floor.

"That's what I was afraid of. Well, if you believe in miracles, we can try. Otherwise we could try plan B."

My fingers shot out and clenched his smooth arm. "Plan B?"

He glanced down. "Cool. Bare skin touching is permitted now? And, of course, I have a plan B. Check out the Jeep's back window."

I craned my head. The top half of a bicycle jostled against the back glass. He'd somehow stuck a bicycle on the rear of his vehicle.

He rattled on as if deaf to my groan. "You need us to be in two places, so we'll split up. You practically have the bike riding thing down already. We'll pull over and let you practice pedaling while I write down your directions for home. Once you have the hang of balancing and steering, I'll drive to this place in Portland to deliver your message while you pedal home to your family. Bing, bang, boom, done. Disaster averted."

He placed a hand on my head to stop its rotating.

"It's cake. You're dressed normal, and you'll make it home within a few hours, as long as you stick to the roads. That's important. No shortcuts into the safety of national forests or nothing. Quit saying no! You can't let your hate for bikes stop you."

"It's not that, it's...well, read this." I pulled the grungy, sweat-marked paper out, unfolded it, and thrust it at him.

Between the glances he spared for the road, he read Ruth's note to Rahab's Roof. It fluttered onto my lap. "I see. The description of you as the messenger. Even if I could somehow obtain full body tattoos, I couldn't pull off—"

"Being a girl?"

"The hostile demeanor. That's all you. But yeah, the girl thing is a hurdle as well. So, okay, you have to go to this Rahab Roof place. We don't split up. And I guess you need to decide. Portland or home?"

I'd known my decision since I'd retrieved my stolen message back. Ruth's task my grandma had accepted was my top priority. Yet announcing this to Wolfe meant giving up on Gilead—that I chose to let him become a murderer in order to save hundreds of other Christians from that same fate.

My chest ached, a reminder of my brother's rib-cracking squeeze the night I'd returned home last fall, communicating his love. Gilead loved me. Even though he'd never in our whole lives said the words.

I touched my ear. Every dawn for three months last spring, I'd awaken to an acorn projectile stinging the outer rim. After I'd swung, yawning, to the frosted forest floor, Gilead, impatient and fingering backup acorns, had forced my weak, stringy body to exercise. Over time he'd made me tougher. He'd taught me survival for my trek through enemy territory. "Dad's gone, Dove. But I'm not. I won't let nothing hurt you. I promise."

I had never promised him that I'd protect him back. But it had been implied.

I'm sorry, brother.

Wolfe reached over and patted my head like I'd seen him do with Jezebel. "To Portland, then."

My eyes blurred the wilderness into relentless green on either side of the winding road to the city. As the blueness of a lake flashed by, I lurched forward in my seat, thrown by the Jeep's abrupt stop.

Wolfe reversed us so we rolled backward on the pavement a few yards. He slow-whistled a long note. "Dove? Billboard at two o'clock. Check it out."

While he maneuvered the car onto a stretch of dirt at the edge of the forest, I blinked to clear my vision. Only the sight of my own face, magnified a hundred times, could have shocked me out of mourning for my brother.

On a huge sign stuck in front of some larches, my tanned, sweaty features glared out over the road to beyond the lake. As if noticing mere people in a Jeep wasn't worth my time. My chopped blonde hair fanned in a frozen, half arc behind me. Below my neck and against the beige Texan dirt, rectangular, blood-red words spelled out FANATIC SURVIVING, followed by numbers, date and time.

"Whoa. You're famous. So famous. Look how giant your head is—they don't make a nobody's head that big. These ads cost a fortune. And it looks like someone else noticed you're a big deal, too."

Distracted by my giant picture, I hadn't noticed Uncle Saul until Wolfe waved up. My relative balanced on a narrow ledge to the side of my tilted chin.

I opened the door and hurtled forward into the tree line. "We found him, your lost boy—Zechariah Brae. He's alive, living on Mount Washington, and he's totally fine. Well," my head bobbled searching for more truthful words "as fine as a Brae can be. The betraying creep. So you can stop searching for him and come home now."

My uncle froze on the larch he descended. Wolfe held out the electronic he sometimes fiddled with. "She's right. See? Here's a picture of him."

My uncle's boots touched the ground's needles, and his hand with the black-rimmed nails wrapped around the offering. He stared at the picture of Zech. When he released the electronic, Wolfe snatched it before it hit the ferns.

Half-hidden by beard, my uncle's lips worked for a few seconds. "Safe?"

"Yeah, he's fine, Saul. Totally safe."

"Home?"

"Yes, please, Uncle. Come home."

"Hang on." Wolfe steered me a few feet away.

"What!?" I ripped my elbow away and kept my eyes glued to my relative. It was only a matter of minutes until he decided to slip away, his usual method of departure. Walking even a few feet from him like this was a risk.

"Dove, look at me. This is important. Do you think your uncle is capable of delivering the message to your brother on his own? In case we don't make it back by midnight? I mean we could write it down and give him the bike to ride and—hey! Be careful!"

In the five seconds I focused on Wolfe, Saul had relocated to the inside of the Jeep. He sat in Wolfe's usual spot up front.

Wolfe studied my uncle. He grunted as I rejected his idea about my uncle contacting my family in time...and how Gilead wouldn't believe him. "Sure, sure, Dove. Forget it. But can he drive?"

"Yes. I drive. Very well."

Uncle Saul's unexpected reply stopped my breath in my throat. I turned and met Wolfe's questioning face. "He's not lying. He can drive."

My grandpa could drive, and he'd taught my dad and uncle the skill when they were boys. Grandpa had also said "no good had come of it" when Gilead hinted long ago at being taught.

Long fingers gripped my shoulders, which I didn't shake off. "Listen, Dove. New plan. I think it's a better one. If you really trust your uncle—and this is up to you—then what if he drives you to Portland so you can talk to the people at Rahab's Roof? And I'll ride the bike to your property. I can deliver your message to your family for you. They know who I am."

"But...no! No, my brother tried to kill you last time you came onto our property. He stabbed you. And he's going to be all pumped about the Reclaim tomorrow. He doesn't like you in any case because he thinks I...that I—"

Wolfe flashed his teeth. "And that's why I'll risk a visit."

I launched myself at him. For once, Wolfe wasn't an idiot and kept quiet.

I let go of his waist and spoke to the pinprick holes of his shirtfront. "But if you die, Wolfe..." My only selfish reason for choosing to drive to Portland first— my personal silver lining on this storm of tragedy— was that I got to keep Wolfe with me, out of my brother's reach tonight.

With this new plan, I would hand-deliver him to my brother. And the Picketts didn't know God. His death and eternity meant something much different than my brother's.

My heart beat faster, marking the few precious seconds I had left to make a difference in this nonbeliever's eternity. "Wolfe, you saw the miracles—fire and wind—a couple weeks ago too, right? You're smart enough to recognize God's work? Before you go, why don't you—"

But he'd turned away, his features transformed with an odd expression. Pumped that I'd broken my no-touching rules on him again? Amazed? He cupped his hands to his mouth. "Saul? Hey, Mr. Saul Strong. Are you serious you can drive your niece here to—"

"Portland." Saul shifted his hand from the wheel, and the engine turned on.

"You know, I think he can do it."

I nodded. The news that Zech Brae had been discovered unhurt had flipped a switch inside my uncle's brain. The man could function and speak again.

Go.

Through the forest silence, the beacon that'd led me in Shafter, Texas, whispered to me again. It directed me into the Jeep, wanting me to go with my uncle to Rahab's Roof. God was faithful. He would lead. He had healed my uncle.

Yet I had failed. I had wasted all those long hours when we'd been cooped up in the Jeep together. Why hadn't I demanded Wolfe take immediate action to change his eternity? Why hadn't I forced Rebecca to talk with him about salvation? The girl could talk a sparrow into believing it was an eagle if she tried. My fingers dug into my cheeks.

"Rebecca!"

Wolfe whipped around. *Clatter crash.* The bicycle he'd been lowering to the ground fell over with a bounce. "Where?"

"No, I mean you can call Rebecca and have her come with you to talk with my family. Better yet, you stay off my property and let her give the message to them alone. Just show her where I live, and she can do the rest."

"I can't, Dove."

"Don't be brainless. It's the perfect solution. She'll be in less danger than you since she's a Christian. She can deliver it in Amhebran, and they'll believe her because, you know, everyone does."

He eased the bicycle upright, straightening the handle bars. "No. I mean I can't ask her to come with me to your property because she's gone...I don't know where. And I don't know how to reach her. She gave herself away by defending you so much back at the CTDC. At least, she made your prosecutor suspicious. Last night, she told me she had to relocate with her family. They'll be in danger now that people have guessed she's a fanatic. She junked her phone, too. I found out this morning when I called her. Rebecca's out. She can't help us."

Lines on his forehead appeared when he spoke of Rebecca's departure, even though he gave the skinny tire an energetic whirl. I stashed my hands behind my back so he wouldn't see them shake and think I was scared for any of us.

I wasn't scared. Only my hopes had skyrocketed and plummeted so fast, my adrenaline now fired at random, making me weak.

Hooonk! Honkhonkhonk!

Wolfe shot a suspicious glare at the back of my uncle's scraggly head. "Hmm. He seems eager to be driving again...to be driving my Jeep. Don't let him take it off road or do anything crazy, though, you promise, Dove? And tell him I want my ride back. You hear that, Mr. Saul Strong? I want my Jeep returned when you guys are finished in Portland."

Honk! Honk!

He stood and moved as close as he could without touching me. His hand shot out, as if to grasp my shoulder again, but he jammed it through his shaggy hair. His final instructions flew out like the beating of a hummingbird's wings. "You have him drive straight to your property when you're finished, and I'll be there waiting for you. Be careful in Portland. I won't be there to explain to people who don't understand that you're all right...for a fanatic freak. And Dove? Between me and Stone?"

"Why choose? You're both idiots."

"Yeah, but who's the biggest idiot? Tell me."

I pointed.

He pumped his fist in victory. "I'd better go. I've got to stop off at the store first, to do some shopping."

Shopping? He was going to stop and buy chips now?

He smirked at my sniff. "Shopping to pick up a new radio. In case, well, in case your big bro won't listen to me. Just make sure you do your part. Get your fanatic message for peace on the radio, and he'll be OK."

My arms flew up to hug him again. Instead, I wrapped them around my own waist.

With a chuckle, he turned, mounted the bicycle,

and pedaled away. A whistled tune carried back to my ears. "Jesus Loves Me."

Could the solution be that simple? Buy another radio? Assuming that Wolfe knew where to find one because I had no clue. And Wolfe's true meaning in buying the electronic?

The radio was a backup. Plan C.

In case my brother silenced Wolfe before he had time to speak.

32

My uncle aimed the headlights at an open space in the barbed wire fence. The lit-up, gnarled edges of the hole looked as if a cow-sized rat had gnawed its way through. With screeching of steel against steel, he eased the Jeep through. The headlights illuminated the black pavement beyond.

The rectangular tower we approached pressed the night sky. Hundreds of identical, evenly spaced windows reflected tonight's odd, red moonlight. My spine pressed further into the seatback while I spared a glance for the other shorter buildings inside the fence enclosure. I'd lost my beacon hours ago, but my uncle drove as if he knew where to go, toward the structure that dominated the landscape and loomed like an old growth among saplings.

The engine quit. The foreign, cement landscape pulsated with danger from the Heathen-created structures. I sat in the prickling stillness, half turned for the space behind my seat. Only a two-second crawl over the upholstery, and I could pull the familiar, musty tarp over my head.

Uncle Saul tapped the grimy paper stuck between my damp palms, interrupting my plan to hide. I nodded and lingered, toying with the idea of staying put. Couldn't whoever I needed to speak to—this Rahab person—come to me? I mean, I'd come ninety-nine percent of the way.

One measly percent, Lord?

My uncle tugged the message I clutched, creating a weird tug-of-war. "Rahab's Roof. In Portland. Here."

Oh, fine.

Abandoning the comparable safe haven of Wolfe's Jeep, I crept after him onto the cracked, cigarette-butt littered blacktop. The tobacco-stained paper was evidence that the Enemy's workers had been here and could still be anywhere. Behind the pyramid of wooden crates. Around the corner of the tall building. Or on the other side of the covered garbage bin.

He led us nearer the bin, the kind I'd been hiding in when he'd rescued me last August. But how did he know where to go? Had he visited Rahab's Roof before? For hours without incident, he'd maneuvered us through lines of vehicles to this spot, but what if he was wrong now? What if he had lapsed back to his not-so-sane decision making? The kind that led to violent Heathen?

I paused and secured my Armor of God around me. Tightening my protection. Making sure there were no chinks.

OK, no more fear, Dove. God's got this.

I'd left my backpack in the Jeep, so I shoved the folded paper I gripped deep into my sock. I kneeled and then wormed my body after my uncle's into the inky gap under the covered bin.

There was just enough space for me to crawl without my stomach scraping the ground. Muted, dragging noises registered from nearby in the darkness. Probably it was only our knees and tops of our shoes, scuffing against the rough pavement. Not snakes. Not rodents with gnawing, sharp teeth. I rested a moment on my belly and thrust my sword and shield arms out in front of myself. They met nothing.

"Here. It's here." Uncle Saul's wiry arm guided me to where he'd twisted onto his back. His hands worked at a spot on the cool metal. Something scraped. He thrust up with an exhaled grunt. Four times he shoved.

The hidden door came ajar with a rusty groan. My uncle pushed up again. There were whispers, as if the contents in the bin above shifted and slid away. A black square overhead yawned with a diameter less than the length of my arm.

Uncle Saul prodded me. "Climb."

I eased up and then clambered all the way into the garbage bin enclosure, kneeling on cardboard. My nose still didn't detect a trace of garbage, only the aroma of old boxes and papers.

While I waited for my uncle to pull himself up, I got to my feet and touched the solid plastic above my head. The lid was tightly secured. It wouldn't budge. I swung my fist upward, but I fought my instinct. Hammering might alert evil passersby to our position.

My body dropped and scooted for the trap door, but my uncle blocked my exit.

"Shoosh. Shoosh." He shepherded me away from him. I stayed in front, shuffling, climbing, and sliding by feel through the cardboard obstacles until solid steel rose against my palms.

I banged it once. "Saul? Saul?"

"Up."

His hands clenched around my waist. With his sudden boost, my scalp bumped the lid, which caused my body to double over. My flailing hands caught the edges of a wide hole. It felt like the end of a square, metallic tunnel in the wall.

I wriggled inside the tube, a tight, slippery, uphill squeeze. In a few short seconds, I arrived at its other end and lowered myself down onto the hard ground.

A harsh chemical smell assaulted my nose. Even though I was as blind as I'd been in the bin of cardboard, I knew I was inside the tower building. I groped in an arc with my fingers and connected with a long-handled tool.

Crash.

I lurched aside and knocked over what sounded like a hollow bucket.

"Shh."

When my uncle moved past, my hands clutched the air behind, as if to hold onto his filthy shirt and not let go. He cracked open a door. Gloom replaced the darkness.

I picked my way over the fallen mop and stepped through the doorway after him into an empty hall with stretched windows. In the eerie moonlight, my narrowed eyes searched for a sign that would direct me to Rahab's Roof Radio Broadcasting. But I was being brainless. If one existed, it would never be visible in this area of the building.

The polished slate floors, decorative window grilles, and fitted river-rock wall sections didn't belong to my people. These details spoke of money and wastefulness...traits from the Enemy's side. No, there'd be no hint of the Christians I'd climbed through a garbage bin for in this section of building.

Did a group of Jesus's followers actually use this enemy building to deliver radio messages to the Oregonian believers? If so, how were they not discovered? Captured?

Rebecca lived here in Portland, next door to

nonbelievers. Or at least she used to. How had I never realized how brave she was? To eat, sleep, and live every hour with the devil's workers within spitting distance?

"Uncle Saul? Do you know where—"

"Up." He stomped down the hall away from me. Each slamming footfall echoed down the posh corridor. "Oh when the saints! Go marching in! When the saints go marching in! Oh Lord, I want to be in that number! When the saints go..."

After three heart-pounding seconds of frozen shock, I fled in the opposite direction. Away from Saul. I had to put distance between me and my uncle who belted out his hymn for no apparent reason. It was like watching him claim the yellow line on a vehicle-occupied road all over again.

My shoe soles thudded down the slick floor and skidded around a corner. Further down the hall, a door slammed.

Hide.

I darted through an open doorway to my right. The room was empty except for monstrous furniture and another stretched window. I smashed against the wall and slithered to the floor. The enthusiastic song about saints grew fainter.

Someone panted past my doorway. Another pair of running feet pursued. A stranger's voice yelled. Still, my uncle's song persisted in his booming alto.

Then the hymn cut off. There were shouts, but I couldn't make out words.

I need to get out of here! No, I need to stay hidden. Don't think about Uncle Saul and what's happening to him. Calm down.

I counted to twenty, sucking in and blowing out

slow breaths. No one else moved past the room where I hid. I exhaled and twisted around the fancy doorframe that stood identical to all the others running the length of the corridor. How was I supposed to figure out where to go? The only object that broke the expensive hallway's monotony was a glowing sign at its end: STAIRS.

I threw up my hands. *Show me, Lord. Help me find the people I need to get to.*

A second later I sprinted for the door under the green sign.

Sky alive, how could I have missed it? My uncle had said "Up."

33

I hesitated on the top stair to catch my breath. My fingers gripped beneath my ribs, squeezing away the side ache. I had no time for it.

Saul said I was supposed to go up. I'd climbed forty flights of stairs...now what?

The gray ceiling didn't reveal the outline of another hidden door or hatch like the one my uncle had found in the floor of the cardboard bin. But I needed to get to the roof, at least to rule it out. How?

Frustration blurred my eyes. I swiped at them. No time for that. On about the twentieth set of stairs, I'd realized why my uncle had reverted to his crazy ways, singing and attracting attention. He'd sacrificed himself for me. He'd known pagan humans patrolled the building at night. He'd drawn them to himself in order to leave the rest of the building safer for me to explore so I could find Rahab's Roof.

I wouldn't waste a second of his sacrifice.

I yanked open the handled door in the wall and stepped into an empty hall.

The corridor was identical to the one where I'd left Saul, except this one was dusty, as if people didn't come up this way much. I hurried along the slate floors, and I passed a straining black garbage bag against a wall of stacked river rock. My head swiveled, not wanting to miss a sign or clue.

Should I try these doors? Would the radio station be behind one?

I paused at a long window, pressing my face to it. There was nothing suspicious on the roof that I could see, and I was at the top of the building. I was as "up" as far as I could go inside this tower. If the people I searched for were located indoors, this was where they'd be. If this was the correct location...

I tried a door to my left. It refused to open. The next one was also locked. I clutched handles and threw my shoulder against each door. Then I rounded the corner.

A sea of doors awaited me. What seemed like thousands of elegant wood rectangles lined both sides of the long hallway. I doubled over as if I'd been punched.

I spat on my hands and rotated my shoulder blades, preparing myself. I dismissed the first door, a metal one. A sign declared it an emergency exit, and an alarm would sound if I opened it. A siren. The last thing I needed.

But then I turned to face it. I listened for a moment. Nodded. And shoved the handle hard. The door swung open as if it had dust-caked hinges. I stepped forward into a stairwell, identical to the one I'd left.

Somewhere below, an earsplitting alarm pealed.

34

Above my head, two strands of faded yellow plastic crisscrossed in an X.

Caution.

The printed word repeated itself from end to end on the ribbons pulled over the piece of plywood that covered a rectangular hole in the ceiling. The weathered, ugliness of the board sat like an eyesore in the lavish perfection of the rest of the building. It smacked of Christians.

The blaring siren crippled my brain, killing any plan I might have had when I decided to open this door. Instead of moving to get to the hole in the ceiling, I studied the flight of stairs going down, identical to the set I'd raced up minutes ago. How long would it take the guards to run forty flights? Five minutes? Six?

Ice slithered over me. I remembered something terrible. Elevators. Vehicles in tall buildings, like this one, that delivered riders to the spot they desired within seconds. I'd never seen an elevator, but I'd been told about them.

I launched myself up toward the covered hole, missed it by a foot, and thudded back onto the painted concrete. Stumbling, I rescued myself at the top stair and teetered on its edge. The possible entrance to the roof was too high. I, a tree climber, the girl who outclimbed Stone Bender, needed a boost.

There was a rail attached to the cream-colored

wall. In an awkward maneuver, I attempted to get my toes on it like a foothold. I slipped off. As I gripped the bar on the other side in a second attempt, something slapped me on the cheek.

I cringed away from the light blow. My hands batted, then closed around, a decent sized rope. It dangled from the opening where the board had vanished and the sky appeared.

I tugged. The rope held my weight.

Hand over hand, I climbed for the night sky. I climbed as if the men who had surrounded my uncle were at my heels. Only when I flung onto the tar roof, did I realize the siren had stopped.

A hand grabbed my arms and wrestled them back. With a rustling of plastic, someone I couldn't see pulled me to my feet. A sharp edge pressed against my throat.

"Why do you seek the roof?"

I threw my elbows back, connecting with the solid torso of the person behind me. "Quit fooling around and sheath your knife! You're wasting time! We've got to get the new Reclaim decision on the radio right now. What time is it?"

The stranger in a black plastic poncho flung me away. "You speak Amhebran? Why clothe yourself like a Heathen?"

I yanked my shoe partway off and fumbled in my sock. My fingers slapped the paper into the woman's unreaching hand that protruded from the giant garbage sack she wore over her clothes. "Read it. Hurry up. And what time is it?"

The woman with heavy eyebrows didn't reply but gestured to a towering pile of cement with her knife. "Hey, Danny? Better get over here. We've got a possible messenger from the Council. She claims to have brought us a new Reclaim decision."

"Righto." Another figure in black stepped out from behind a cement chimney-like structure with a tall metal antennae rising out of it. The oversized bag he wore like a poncho caught the strong breeze. His light frame flapped over to join the woman holding Governor Ruth's message.

Their eyes traveled back and forth across the paper then lifted to me. I held up my inked arms for them and scowled at their slowness.

"Tattoos. Hostile demeanor. Check and check. Not sure why she's clothed in that getup...but where's messenger one?" She lifted the paper out to the reddish moonlight and squinted. "Where's the other female? 'Eighty-two years of age, 5 foot 3 inches, with an identifying scar running wrist to elbow'?"

"Dead. Died. My grandma died. Now, you'd better get on with it—announce the changed outcome for peace before more people die. What time is it?"

"Nine thirty-two. Danny? Better send this as an alert on the waves and keep it rolling through tomorrow night. Roll it out to Seattle, too, if you can get it that far, just in case. Haven't heard from them lately, so it goes to figure their messenger might not have delivered, and they don't know. That or their signal's weak."

"Righto." His garbage-bagged body sailed around a corner. I assumed he headed to a different part of the roof where he kept his radio equipment to broadcast.

She slapped the flat part of her knife against her palm a couple more times. "Well, messenger two, you didn't give us much time to announce this switch in our holy war uprising. I won't lie. Last week would've been better. You have a bad time finding this roof? Because I didn't realize the Council knew our new location."

"They don't. At least, they didn't tell me if they do."

"Then I guess they picked the right messenger. Finding us must have been like spotting the lucky pigeon splat on an overpass. And that's sorry news about your grandma." She stuck out her hand. "The name's Rahab Rae. Welcome to my roof and broadcasting station. I'd say make yourself at home, but we're not set up for visitors. And you're...?"

"Dove."

"Don't give out your last name?"

"I do. Just lost track of which one I use now." My thighs trembled under my palms that braced against them, as though I'd outrun a swarm of hornets. But I'd choose wasps or hornets rather than patrolling Heathen any night. How could a Christian stay in this concrete world, a place without trees, bees...or any of the nature God created? Even a locust-chewed, Texas wasteland was preferable to this. I moved nearer the rope whose frayed end looped a cement piece of the roof.

"Uh, Danny to Rahab. This is Danny. You hear me over there, Rahab?"

"Like an air horn."

"Righto. Well, we've got a situation."

Rahab scampered up and around some cinder blocks and a pile of broken metal as agile-footed as a tree dweller. "What kind of situation, Danny?"

"The not-so-good kind of situation. Hard to explain."

He was wrong. As soon as we rounded the corner

and got hit by the blast of wind that lifted my hair at its roots, the situation was obvious.

Danny held out hands that no longer held Ruth's message. His plastic bag cracked in the air around him, and his head bandana must've blown away, too, because his long hair flapped like angry ropes. "I'm sorry to report...it's gone. A thousand apologies, messenger two."

The message-stealing wind pummeled our motionless bodies. Then Danny's arm shot out at the wooden crate whose top supported a jumble of techy-looking stuff. He snatched at a falling black, cattail object—a miniature of the microphone Lobo and Jessica had chased me with.

From behind the crate, another bulging bag sprang up. A guy Gilead's age wearing a garbage disguise made a grab at some other equipment with cords that teetered in the gusts. After rescuing it, he turned his gaze on me. His grizzled chin jutted. "W-w-wait. I know you. You were at the Council. The Heathen lover."

All three garbage-bagged Christians continued to scrutinize me as I struggled to brace myself against the wind and his accusation.

"Reunions later. Radio first." Rahab steered me through the gusts to where the jumbled equipment waited. "Hope you memorized your message, delivery girl, because you're all of it we've got left. A hint, don't be the Queen of England with the mic. Our people need to hear the truth, not fancy phrases."

My feet tangled on a cord. "Wait, what? I'm not...but you read it, too! Danny? Rahab? Both of you did, I saw you. So, one of you announce it."

"I skimmed on the middle part. Danny, you

remember details on Ruth's orders? Enough to report on it?"

"That's a negative. Messenger two, you're up."

"Not microphone shy?" She released my elbow and leaped over to the metal tower.

Something clamped over my head like ear muffs. Danny's stubborn hands didn't allow mine to rip them off while the other Christian fiddled with a complicated electronic on the wooden crate. With a grudging nod, the grizzled chin gestured that I hunker behind the crate. Once I ducked, the wind's clawing lessened.

Rahab tapped my hair. Her wide mouth moved in Amhebran, "You're on. Portland's listening. Speak what you remember. Keep it simple."

"I...I..."

Ruth's message refused to come out in Amhebran or English. Seconds ago, each word of the missive had burned like fire inside my skull. Now I couldn't remember any of it. The wind had blown her sentences out of my head like it had blown the important paper out of Danny's grasp.

I sat with an empty mind, like an idiot, babbling to Portland's smoggy air.

Words, God, please...

Flinging down beside me, Danny grabbed the microphone from my hands. "Righto, Oregon listeners. This is Danny D from Rahab's Roof with an urgent message from the Councils. Here with me is...?" His elbow dug into me.

Who am I? My name is...uh... "Dove."

His long-haired, ear-muffed head bobbed. "Dove is the chosen messenger of the Oregon Council. And let me tell you folks, she sacrificed a lot to get here, including her grandmother's life. I trust her, and I challenge you to do so as well. So, Dove, tell us about this critical news we need to hear. Is it regarding a changed Reclaim answer?"

"I...I..." My eyes pleaded with his. He had brown irises. Like Jezebel's and Wolfe's. And Lobo's. I was here to make sure Lobo's brown eyes didn't become lifeless and unseeing. With the force of a flood breaking a dam, the words from Rahab's message came tumbling out.

While I announced the new spiritual versus physical aspect of our war, I chanced a glance past the concrete roof, to the horizon where dots of light marked people's presences. They were people who wanted to lock up and hurt Christians. People my brother wanted to kill. And people like Wolfe...Wolfe who'd already been stabbed once by a Christian.

Danny leaned over to take the microphone I'd accepted back. I clenched it in both hands and twisted it out of his reach. My shoulders curled over.

"Don't sin. C'mon, people! Help me frustrate Satan by winning souls for Christ."

I shouted at Portland below. My words joined the wind and sailed out beyond the city to the state's seacoasts, forests, and farmlands. "Don't kill our enemies. Save them. Because they're not our enemies! I know you think they are, but they aren't! Get to know them. Care about their eternities and protect them. And so what if others in your family call you a Heathen lover? Only cowards and weak-minded minions care what others think—"

Danny ripped the cattail object away. "You've just heard from Dove, messenger for the Oregon Council. If you only tuned in a second ago, we'll be replaying this emergency alert for the next thirty-six hours...possibly." He shook his head at me.

Rahab had disappeared around the metal tower.

Doubled over against the wind, I fought my way for the tall structure. The moonlight washed my cement surroundings red as it had in my dream. If the dream progressed along its course, a tremendous earthquake would hit any second, and the building under my soles would melt into a pile of rubble.

"Oof!" I slammed into the solid chest of someone in a garbage bag.

The Christian with the stutter who remembered me from the Council trapped me tight against the black plastic he wore. "I should throw y-you off our roof for that stunt you pulled. Then we'd see if those pagans that love you so m-m-much catch you at the bottom."

"Grow some ears. I never said they love me."

"You think what we do up here is a joke? We don't risk our lives every day so you can waste our time and the airwaves with a fake Council message the night before the Reclaim. I'm going to fill Danny in on who you are. And when I'm done, if you're s-s-still loitering...let's just say you'll find out firsthand how long it takes to fall five hundred and fifty feet."

I wrested myself free.

Rahab was waiting for me around the other side of the cement chimney structure. Her unsheathed knife dangled from her fingers. "That was some message you delivered. I don't remember reading all of that on the missive from Ruth."

The breeze blew cold on my hot cheeks. "I said it as I remembered it."

"Hmm. You in such a hurry to go?" She led me past a pile of weathered boards. We ended up on a side of the building I hadn't yet seen. Bird droppings riddled a cement wall that stood otherwise empty, except for a lone, gray, handleless door.

"I'll say your good-byes to Danny for you. You're right. Best to avoid confrontations on my roof. A bit risky up so high—it leads upset humans into certain temptations. And, here, wear this on your way out."

Her blade ripped a line in an oversized black garbage sack identical to what she wore over her dark clothes. She handed it to me. "If any security hunters get within earshot, you duck down and ball up inside of this. Stay still, hold your breath, and they won't notice you except to comment that the janitors are getting behind on trash removal."

The gray door slid open.

Sky alive! She wanted me to ride an elevator? "Rahab, I'll exit the other way and use the rope—"

She yanked the garbage bag over my head and propelled me forward. My head poked out from a slash in the plastic in time to find myself in a small empty space no bigger than an outhouse.

She blocked my escape back to the roof. "Ride the elevator to the basement. It opens to the kitchens, which is a construction zone, so watch your step. You'll find your exit against the south wall next to the storage room."

"I...I can't ride this thing! It's not safe—with the earthquake."

She raised her caterpillar brow at my stuttered objection and pushed a 'B' on the wall in front of me. "What earthquake? Shalom, messenger Dove. You're a strange one. Perhaps I'll understand you better when we meet again in our Father's House. Until then." She saluted, the door shut, and the floor under my feet lurched and fell.

~*~

I poised in the semidarkness, ready to run. The yawning room I stepped into from the elevator echoed with my breathing. The shadows suggested metal surfaces and sharp corners.

Hide in Me. I Am your refuge.

Plodding footsteps approached from the right. A dim light grew until a flashlight beam swept over the black garbage bag I cowered in. It lit up the thin plastic over my face, then passed on. The footsteps faded, and I breathed when darkness swallowed me again.

I threw off my disguise. Ruth had said the elevator led to the kitchens, which would then exit to the outside. And on the outside pavement I'd find the Jeep.

What would I do if I made it to Wolfe's ride? I couldn't drive myself or wait under the tarp in the back for someone to help me. No one knew where I was. No one was left to help me except God.

Thank You for sheltering me.

I shoved aside the worry as my hands did the same to the plastic film draped over the drywall. The sweaty heel of my hand pressed cool metal of a doorframe. With a two-handed shove, the door swung open.

I sprinted into the moon's eerie light while my feet stumbled in my hurried tiredness. Ahead, the lone Jeep waited where I'd left it in front of the fence line.

Without slowing, I rubbed my blurry eyes. Why couldn't I erase the image of a person sitting in the front of the vehicle? The combined stress and exhaustion had broken my mind. The hallucination in the Jeep refused to melt away.

Uncle Saul started the engine and beckoned me to join him inside.

35

I awoke with a jerk that unstuck my cheek from the Jeep's glass. As I rubbed the skin, the numbers of the clock glowed 1:30 AM.

May fifteenth. Reclaim Day had begun. Had my family—my brother—heard the radio message I'd delivered in Portland? Had they believed Governor Ruth and me? Had they obeyed?

Had Rahab and Danny even broadcasted it?

I swiveled to question Uncle Saul, who maneuvered us around a curve in the road. But I refaced the side window. My uncle hadn't said a word since I'd discovered him waiting for me in Wolfe's ride. I'd questioned him on his escape. How had he gotten away? But I might as well have asked his boots.

The glow of an approaching town lit the blackness of pines. An illuminated wooden sign sped into sight. *Welcome to Sisters.* Around its base, flowers flourished in manicured lines like spokes on a wheel, the way nonbelievers grew them.

My nose pressed the cool glass at the sign we passed. "Whoa, Uncle Saul. We're not supposed to be here. Remember? Wolfe's not home here in Sisters. He's waiting for us back at our home in Ochoco. Turn us for Prineville instead. Hurry."

He continued to drive us past the wooden, western-themed buildings, whose inside lights stayed off.

"Uncle. Listen to me. Detouring through Sisters is a terrible idea. Not to mention pointless, a waste of time, and—"

His swift, fierce look shut me up. I pounded my palm in frustration against the edge of the seat next to me. My movements knocked a paper to the car's floor. *Vehicle Registration*. Wolfe's name and home address ran below the title in black print.

"He's not here, Uncle."

I bit my tongue. I wasn't scared of my dad's brother, but I couldn't help but squirm when his glare jabbed me like that.

~*~

I scrunched down in my seat and shook my head to communicate how dumb it was to park in front of the Picketts' home. My uncle traveled the short footpath alone to the door in the familiar home. From the inside of the Jeep, I scanned the property for obvious signs of a recent attack. Had any of my people visited this area of Sisters?

The grass stretched taller and greener now. But I saw no broken windows. No smoke. No cop cars. The homes still loomed the same, oversized and boxy. It didn't appear that any Christians had paid a vengeful, Reclaim visit tonight.

A single footstep gave me warning.

I sat upright, my fingers bruising my forearms with my grip. "Why are you here?"

Jessica, the girl I'd left states away in Texas, opened Saul's door. She slipped onto the empty seat beside me. "Pickett? From Sisters? I figured sooner or later you'd make an appearance at the Pickett household. Though I know you aren't related. Don't worry. For now, I'm choosing not to tell my dad."

"So? Why should I care?"

"He's Lobo's boss." She raised her brow as if expecting me to gasp.

I shrugged. "Like I said. Why are you here?"

My uncle reappeared, holding hands with a smaller figure who pulled away. *Oh, no, no, no...*

Jessica stiffened. "You kidnapping her?"

"No." Wait! Were we?

Jezebel reached down, chucked something from her path into the grass, and galloped at me.

I opened my door. "Go back inside your home, Tough Stuff. Saul made a mistake. You're not coming with us."

The girl huffed, though her round face smiled. She threw her Minnie Mouse bag into the space behind me and followed it in. "You coming to Dove's house, too, Jessica?"

Jessica shook her head and darted out of the Jeep without a word. She kept a ten-foot buffer between herself and my uncle as she moved for the home's front door.

"Wait a sec, Uncle. Don't start the engine yet. Jezebel Pickett, you get out of here. Now."

"Why? Grandma's not home, and Diamond can't tell me what to do. I make my own decisions. And I want to go to where Woof is. This guy that hiked with us last summer says Woof's at your house, and Dove, it's about time you asked me over. True friends visit each other's houses. They even have spend-the-nights. True friends do."

I studied the shadows of nearby doorways. My

muscles tensed, preparing to see Jessica reappear, joined by another small but eviler figure I dreaded. "Jezzy, you said Diamond can't tell you. Why would she care or have a say in what you do?"

"Stop worrying so much! She's asleep. I know 'cause I saw her breathing all slow on the couch since she's spending the night over. Grandma's having a late night out in Bend. My grandma calls it a "get out and breathe or bust" night. Anyway, I wrote down that I'd come back soon and stuck it on the espresso maker, so no one'll get all freaked out and call the cops. They just have to learn that I make my own choices where I go." She made a palms-up gesture as if to say, *that's just the way it is.*

I peered over her at the home disappearing behind us. "And you know Jessica?"

"Uh, of course! She's Diamond's cousin."

Sky alive! I should have known. Her stance and build had been Diamond's. But how could I have guessed? Oh, why...with the billions of people on earth...did it have to be Diamond who shared her DNA? And had Rebecca known about the relationship? Somehow, I thought yes. Perhaps that was part of the reason I was chosen so fast after my arrest to be the new girl on *Fanatic Surviving.*

I chewed my thumbnail. "Cousins. Huh. You don't say. She lives in Sisters, too?"

"Boy, you know nothing, Dove. She's from Salem. Her dad's super rich with horses and a limo and runs a TV show."

"Why is she even here? Why come and try to meet me?"

My murmured questions were for myself, but Jezebel stuck her chin over my seatback and replied.

Her tone was serious. "Well, you do weird stuff and talk about God a lot. It's pretty hilarious and not boring. You have answers to things that no one else does. I'm always like, 'What's Dove gonna say next?' Maybe she wants to find out too?"

My mouth tumbled open. So, I was interesting and entertaining. What about the way I blasted her with my truths about God? Had the Spirit prodded her to find me to satisfy her questions? It seemed more likely that Satan prodded. Especially if she was a cousin to Diamond.

As we rolled out of town at walking speed, I kept half an ear on Jezebel's jabbering about Diamond's rich relatives. Until I remembered the rolled-up bag of chips under the seat. I tossed it back to her.

Peace descended, marked by crunching. I pressed my temples.

My uncle had detoured to Sisters for Wolfe's sister. And Jessica, Diamond's cousin, saw us take her.

Even if I could, by some miracle, force my uncle to turn us around and take Jezebel back...and then somehow force the stubborn girl out of the Jeep...in the end I'd risk facing Diamond who babysat inside her home. No, scratch that plan. I'd deal with Wolfe's sister tomorrow after...well, afterward.

"You win, Tough Stuff. You can tag along."

My uncle drove us through stretches of road lined with trees. No police sirens wailed in pursuit, but my fingernails clawed at the seat on either side of my legs. Jessica would call the cops. Wouldn't she? When the pines ran out, the farmland and high desert dominated until we passed through the sleeping town of Prineville, still unfollowed.

The moment I sighted the white, dead tree

marking the edge of our property, I threw open the door and sprinted for the maples.

"Wait up, Dove! I'm your guest!"

I didn't slow. My arms and legs continued to pump as hard as my heart in my chest.

No bell rang to announce my arrival. A bad sign. Terrible. Where was my grandpa tonight? Why wasn't he doing lookout? Where was the rest of my family...Wolfe? *Oh, Wolfe.*

Let them be here.

A voice spoke. It was my own, blaring from the leaves above. I launched myself onto my home's main tree and began to climb. One branch below my family's living quarters platform, my frown relaxed a little. The sentences I'd spoken at Rahab's Roof...I could be pointing my finger at each Christian, charging every soul in our nation to save the unsaved and frustrate Satan.

My voice came from a radio. Wolfe had made it, then! And my family knew of the changed Reclaim...

Instead of whooping, I groaned. A mute, sickly whimper. With my last pull up, my family came into view. And Wolfe.

The sight was nauseating. In a second, I'd thunder so loud, Prineville would have to cover its ears. But now, I froze in shock.

Wolfe dangled upside down from a cedar ceiling beam with his black hair pointing at the floor. Alive or dead? His white shirt pooled down around his armpits, and the exposed, straight, unmoving line of his vertebrae told me nothing, Suddenly, with the desperation of an animal caught in a trap, he squirmed up to reach the rope securing his ankles to the sturdy beam above.

He flopped down in defeat. His body rotated until the profile of his swollen cheek in his purple face became visible.

Across the room, Gilead sat in Grandma's willow-back chair as if it were a throne. His thumb stayed on the point of the hunting knife he held. When he began to hum, the self-satisfied sound triggered my fury. I raced forward to shake my brother and hit his smug face.

But Jezebel beat me to the punch.

36

I gasped. Gilead, with his lightning reflexes and ability to foresee attacks, hadn't stopped her fist in time. Not that her punch fazed him at all—or even her second, which was more of a sloppy slap against his beard. He didn't even glance at her. His eyes stayed on me.

"Heathen attacking. Hide!"

"Climb! Find Grandpa."

"I get to ring the bell!"

My boy cousins' cries from a nearby sleeping porch brought my head around. It whipped back and forth to locate the new danger, but no godless loomed except Jezebel.

Saul froze, unnoticed, in the shadows of the doorway opposite, still positioned on the ladder. He must have carried Jezebel up since she beat me. But where was the threat?

"Wait...Dove? Is...is that you, child?" My mom crept into the room from the eating platform, her hazel eyes narrowed at me.

I was the threat. I wore my camouflage so well my family hadn't recognized me.

"Child!"

She and my aunt converged, but Jezebel held them back with her raised fists and a snarl.

"I don't know who you are yet, ladies, but this is Dove's home, and I won't let you string her up. And you get Woof down. Get him down, you sickos!"

At her command, Trinity and Jovie flew from the sleeping porch and into the room. They connected with the rocker so hard it lurched. My oldest cousin wrestled Gilead's unreleasing hand for his knife, but my youngest held up a rusty blade and lobbed it. "Catch, Trinity!"

Jezebel stamped. "What're the scissors for?"

Trinity shoved the ancient scissors into her waistband. With the agility of a true tree dweller, she boosted herself from the arm of the rocker and grabbed the giant ceiling beam. "I knew you wouldn't like this ugliness, Dove. I told them you wouldn't. It was only supposed to be for a minute. But Micah left to tell his parents about the Reclaim change. And Gilead..."

Hand over hand, her fingertips jammed into the crack between the beam and the roof boards until she reached Wolfe's black shoes. Her tanned nose wrinkled when she glanced down at his face, misshapen and mottled with the whites of his eyeballs showing through slits.

Could he have brain damage from hanging like that?

Trinity hacked at the twine that held him upside down. Crashing headfirst to the ground wouldn't help his remaining gray cells any, so I leaped over. My arms closed around his cool waist.

I stamped like Jezebel. "Come over and help me, Gilead! I can't hold him myself."

"Dove child! What are you doing?"

I didn't release my grip on Wolfe's bare, sweaty skin, even if my mom was pop-eyed at my inappropriate embrace of a nonbeliever.

My brother remained seated, but Jezebel and Jovie

jostled each other, vying for the prime spot to catch him when he fell.

"Stand aside." My uncle stood next to me. The rags covering his arms pulled tight with Wolfe's sudden weight. He lowered the deadweight onto the ground, and I unwound the broken cords from around the black shoes.

"D-dad?" Trinity whispered from overhead.

"Saul?" My mom's eyeballs looked as though they might explode from their sockets.

Someone screamed. "Where? Where is he? Oh, Saul! My Saul!" My aunt flew into the room and launched herself at her husband. After a few blinks he patted her on the back. *There, there.*

Jezebel, squatting next to me, pointed at Uncle Saul but spoke to Jovie. "That's your dad, too?"

My little cousin squinted up at the filthy, bearded face. Her face flooded pink. "I...I guess he must be."

"Lucky!" Jezebel resumed tugging Wolfe's eyelid.

Wolfe's hand batted hers away. "Quit that."

"Woofy!"

He lurched upward to a sit. "What? Why are you here, Jez? Geesh, Dove! Is this what took you so long to get home? I figured you'd stopped for doughnuts, but I knew you'd make it. I knew it! You made it, and we're all alive!"

His huge grin faded. "Well almost. Your family got a little upset when they heard about your gran. Especially your gramps. He took off somewhere, which is how this psycho brother of yours made himself prime torturer."

He chin-gestured at Gilead, still sitting straight backed in the rocker. With his face blank of surprise or joy, he watched Trinity strangle-hug her dad.

Was my brother thinking about our own dad?

Wolfe lowered his voice and leaned in. "But I didn't tell him or anyone about what you've been up to—or how your gran died. I figured you might not want them to know everything."

I took the rough hand streaked with dried blood in mine. The claw marks from the desert cat he'd tackled had scabbed over. "Then getting strung up was your own dumb fault. You shouldn't have told them about my grandma getting killed if you weren't going to explain. Of course they'd want to know how."

"I didn't tell them she died. You did. On the radio."

"Oh. Uh, yeah. Forgot."

"I'm willing to forget your mistake. As long as you don't forget you chose me—over some hulking mountain guy—as your biggest idiot."

I grinned. "You still are. Idiot."

His arm lifted and hovered a second, as if to reach for me. It drew Jezebel into a crushing hug instead. He pressed his beaten, smiling face to the top of her dark hair. "You know the real reason Dove chose me, Jezzy? It's because I'm more pretty."

"Handsomer," she corrected into his white shirt. "Not pretty."

"Yes. I'm more handsomer."

A shadow fell over his swollen cheek.

Gilead loomed over and pulled me to my feet. "We've got some plans to make. Don't forget this is still Reclaim day."

His hand shot out and shoved the side of Wolfe's head so it swerved toward the floor. Mimicking my brother's lightning speed, Jezebel's foot connected with Gilead's kneecap, then with his shin. "Don't. You.

Touch. My. Brother!"

"So where are we going?" With a distinct limp, my brother side stepped out of range of the cycling legs aimed at him.

Was this why Uncle Saul brought Jezebel along? Because she was the only one who could—or would— land a blow on Gilead? My insides warmed with a smile.

My brother tugged my short shirtsleeve, a reminder that it should be longer. "You'll fit right in with our new neighbors, sis. Isn't that what you said on the radio? Some of us get to live among pagans? I'm assuming us means you."

"I'm coming too this time." Trinity ran over to stand next to me.

The room fell silent. My mom gripped the hem of her tunic, the tendons standing out under her tanned skin.

Gilead shrugged. "Sure, cuz. So am I. The thing is...this Spiritual Reclaim? This lay-down-your-weapons, peace thing? It's never going to work. You think moving groups of God-fearing Christians into the middle of demon-possessed pagans with guns will end in anything but war?"

Oh, Lord! Is he right?

I swallowed hard. "Then stay home, Gil. If you can't control your hate. Right, Mom? Uncle Saul?"

"I think—"

"Sky alive, Dove!" Gilead cut off my mom's reply. "You think I'll stay safe at home while you two girls live unprotected in the middle of those animals? Yeah. That's not going to happen. I'm coming. I'll be there to do recon for the war. Knowing the habits of our enemies will make them easier to defeat."

My mom flopped down in the empty rocker like an old woman. Her fingers pressed her lids. "Yes, Gilead will go with you, Dove. For protection. And Trinity...?"

"Yes." Uncle Saul nodded with vigor. "Yes, she goes. Like Jesus. For the Lord Jesus went from one city and village to another, proclaiming and preaching the kingdom of God."

Heads swiveled toward my uncle's Bible talk. My brother nodded. "So? Where to? Which town?"

Jezebel, who—like Jovie—had sat with her face screwed up in confusion during my brother's talk of war, sprang up. "Mine! My town. Sisters! So Dove and I can be neighbors. And she and Wolfe can be—"

Wolfe yanked her down and covered her mouth. He shook his head.

Gilead began to hum. He reached for his knife hilt.

I shook my head, too. "No. Prineville. The three of us—Gilead, Trinity, and I—will settle in Prineville. It's the nearest town."

My brother unsheathed his knife. He held it up to the lantern light in the air above the Picketts' dark heads and squinted. Surveying the blade for nicks or dullness. Still focused, he stuck out his right hand toward Wolfe. It hovered, palm open in the air before him.

Wolfe released his sister and wobbled up. After a loud swallow, he gripped the waiting hand.

Gilead's fingers closed around Wolfe's, squeezing the tanned fingers under the dried blood. "Neighbors."

"Neighbors," Jezebel's brother glared back.

A distant cop car siren grew louder, but the little girl bounced up. She threw her arms around my waist, clueless about the dangers looming on our horizon, the ugly threats we would have to fight out together—or stay peaceful and let conquer us.

"Yay! I did it. Dove, you're moving to Sisters."

Jezebel was right. Since Gilead was physically the strongest and the most pigheaded, he would get his way. We'd relocate to Sisters for the Spiritual Reclaim.

Thank you…

for purchasing this Watershed Books title. For other inspirational stories, please visit our on-line bookstore at www.pelicanbookgroup.com.

For questions or more information, contact us at customer@pelicanbookgroup.com.

Watershed Books
Make a Splash!™
an imprint of Pelican Book Group
www.PelicanBookGroup.com

May God's glory shine through
this inspirational work of fiction.

AMDG

God Can Help!

Are you in need? The Almighty can do great things for you. Holy is His Name! He has mercy in every generation. He can lift up the lowly and accomplish all things. Reach out today.

Do not fear: I am with you; do not be anxious: I am your God. I will strengthen you, I will help you, I will uphold you with my victorious right hand.

~Isaiah 41:10 (NAB)

We pray daily, and we especially pray for everyone connected to Pelican Book Group—that includes you! If you have a specific need, we welcome the opportunity to pray for you. Share your needs or praise reports at http://pelink.us/pray4us

Here's a sneak peek at the next book in the Dove Strong trilogy
Sent Rising

1

My fistful of carrots flopped onto the pasture's dead grass. I paused with the spear's red-stained tip two paces from my heart.

A couple dozen pointed poles and pronged branches stuck out horizontally from the giant juniper bush at the edge of the forest, positioned to impale the unlucky trespasser who stumbled too close. While I'd harvested the summer's early vegetables from Wolfe's backyard, my brother had been busy beefing up Micah Brae's home security.

I scratched the red wooden point with my fingernail. Not blood. Beet juice...from our garden patch.

"Gilead, this paranoia of yours is stupid. We're here to live peaceably with these people. Not skewer them."

His humming dropped off, though he continued to secure another spear. "Don't stand there hollering in the open, Dove. You'll attract the enemy. On second thought, keep hollering. I wouldn't mind trying out his new defensive boundary while it's still light."

Trinity paused in the act of hanging what appeared be a glass wind chime above Micah's prickly doorway. She jingled it at my lifted brow. "Burglar alarm. To wake Micah if anyone tries to sneak in while he's sleeping. Plus, it's the color of smoke."

"And the color of your eyes. Subtle." I snorted. Trinity had strewn reminders of herself everywhere in our neighbor's cramped, juniper-bush dwelling—from a corn silk pillow the exact hue of her hair to duplicates of her tattoos scratched in the forest floor. She'd planted these subliminal messages in hopes that he would stop being blind to the fact that he liked her in the same way that she liked him.

Gilead fastened a spike next to the wind chime. He paused suddenly, and his expression threw daggers at the pole in my hand. "Sky alive, Dove! You didn't dismantle the defensive perimeter I put up at our place, did you?"

"Only a few spears." I didn't add that I'd tried to remove all of them but hadn't been able to wrestle them off the shelter that he, my cousin, and I shared. "You put them up, so you get to take them down."

"Don't be an idiot. We need them intact."

"I'm the idiot? Your perimeter won't stop fire. Arson is our biggest threat."

He bent to straighten a pronged stick. "It's too dry this season for intentional arson. Even the most brainless demon from this town will think twice before turning our shelter into a fireball. They'd burn up their own homes, too."

I couldn't argue. Even now, the brassy sun seared my exposed skin like a cooking fire and stole the moisture from my lips. "Fine, Gil, but your spikes won't stop any dogs. You've positioned them too high."

"My second perimeter—the outer one—will take

care of any dogs or creatures without foot protection. Haven't you noticed the burr rings I've set in the weeds? They begin ten yards out and get thicker the closer you get to our place. The hounds will go limping home if they try to nose around."

I'd spent a painful hour this morning digging a barbed spike-ball out of my palm. My brother had planted the tiny, torturing bits of nature near our front door on purpose? I swung the blunt end of my pole at his shaggy head to thump some sense into him. He caught it without looking.

The glass tinkled above Trinity's upstretched arms. "Not cool, Gil. I had to cut half my braid off to get two burrs out yesterday. Keep it up, and I'll end up looking like her." She thrust a piece of wind chime in the direction of my blonde, chopped-to-shoulder-length hair.

Micah aimed a pair of wistful eyes at me.

I let go of my tug-of-warring pole and pointed in the direction I'd come. "Gilead, you and Trinity should have been waiting at our place today. What if you all missed Uncle Saul when you were messing around here? You were supposed to be on the lookout for him."

"He'd check here at Micah's—or at *his* place—before giving up on finding us. Isn't that where you were? *His* place?"

Gilead meant Wolfe's property. Since relocating to Sisters, he had yet to call my non-Christian friend by name.

I gazed at the treetops to the east, in the direction of my family's out-of-sight home in Ochoco. "Saul said he'd bring us news from home every Saturday. It's been three Saturdays since we saw him...I think."

Gilead shrugged, but Micah disappeared inside his juniper bush.

"Eleven...twelve...thir-thirteen..." His labored counting continued. The Brae guy kept a tally of each day in this enemy territory where we'd agreed to live for a year as part of the Christian Sent.

His dark head poked out and set the wind chime jingling. "Twenty-two. Twenty-two days since Saul's last visit. You're right, Dove. You're absolutely right." He eyed me. A dog wanting a pat from its master.

Gilead secured another horizontal pole to the prickly bough. "Well, did *he* give you any useful information about what could have stopped Saul? Any report of accidents? Wildfires between here and Ochoco? Attacks?"

I shook my head. Wolfe didn't like to relay bad news. What I knew about the famine, high food costs, and the devastating nation-wide drought, I'd learned from his kid sister, Jezebel. She reported information better than our radio back home.

My brother pulled out his hunting knife and began to whittle a branch's tip. "What a good-for-nothing guy. What a worthless, waste of a human—"

"Probably your uncle went crazy again. He probably forgot where you live now." Jezebel popped up from behind a boulder where she'd been spying. "He'll show up when he remembers. But Dove and I'll go ask my brother if he's heard anything...since the rest of you are too chicken to leave your forts to find out."

In three strides, Gilead towered over the girl. He cracked his knuckles. "OK, Spy. Let's find your brother. Now!"

Trinity dropped the vine supporting her glass pieces. "Chill, Gil. She's like five years old. Anyway, my dad's not crazy."

"Who's five?" Jezebel's bottom teeth clamped over her upper lip in a fierce underbite while she rolled to her sandaled feet. The brown grass clump from her hand rained against my brother's earth tone pantleg. "C'mon, Dove."

Trinity came to stand at my shoulder. "I'll come, too. Micah? Want to go check why my dad's delayed?"

"No. No, I'll, uh...I'll finish up here. I'd like to find out what's going on, but I'd better finish the perimeter. The perimeter is the most important part of security. But you could bring me some corn. Or some strawberries."

Strawberries. Trinity's dreamy, wide-set eyes crinkled in a smile. She touched her wrist where years ago she'd inked on the strawberry plant. A matching drawing ran the perimeter of his shelter's floor.

"It's working," she mouthed.

Gilead, gripping a whittled branch, marched through the center of the field with Jezebel instead of slipping through the bordering foliage toward the paved road that led to the Picketts' home. He barreled through a herd of cows, slapping one on its bony rump. *Who's a coward? ...*

To continue reading, grab a paperback copy or download the e-book today